# LOSING KEI
子

# LOSING KEI

子

*Suzanne Kamata*

A Novel

*Leapfrog Press*
*Wellfleet, Massachusetts*

Published in 2008 in the United States by
The Leapfrog Press
P.O. Box 1495
95 Commercial Street
Wellfleet, MA 02667-1495, USA
www.leapfrogpress.com

Distributed in the United States by
Consortium Book Sales and Distribution
St. Paul, Minnesota 55114
www.cbsd.com

First Edition

Library of Congress Cataloging-in-Publication Data

Kamata, Suzanne.
  Losing Kei : a novel / by Suzanne Kamata. – 1st ed.
    p. cm.
  ISBN 978-0-9728984-9-2
  1. Women artists–Fiction. 2. Americans–Japan–Fiction. 3. Interracial
marriage–Fiction 4. Culture conflict–Fiction. 5. Marital conflict–Fiction. 6. Custody of children–Fiction. 7. Japan–Fiction. I. Title.
  PS3611.A465L67 2007
  813'.6–dc22

                                                          2007029259

for Jio

I would like to thank the editors of *New York Stories, Literary Mama* and *Her Circle Ezine,* where some segments of this novel were originally published in slightly different form. Also a big *domo arigatou gozaimasu* to those who read and commented upon earlier drafts of this work, especially Pat Tanjo, Melinda Tsuchiya, Margaret Stawowy, Noemi Hiraishi, Diane Nagatomo, Colleen Sheils, Joan Itoh Burk, Helene Dunbar, Wendy Jones Nakanishi, Andy Couturier and Maretha Mino. Thanks to Louise Nakanishi-Lind for friendship and advice on surfing; Cynthia Kingsbury for inspiration; Tracy Slater for inviting me to read at Four Stories Japan; Caron Knauer for her patience, passion and persistence; and Yukiyoshi Kamata for indulgence. Further thanks goes to my parents, for never once suggesting I consider a fallback career; Michiyo Kamata and Yukiyo Maegawa for logistical support; and to Jio and Lilia Kamata, my most dependable muses, for just being you. This book wouldn't exist if not for Ira Wood and the good people at Leapfrog Press; thank you for invaluable editorial suggestions and for publishing this novel. Finally, my deepest gratitude goes to the readers of this book.

# LOSING KEI

子

# 1997

I'M AT THE PLAYGROUND, SITTING ON A SWING. THERE'S A TEMPLE next door and from time to time the suggestion of incense wafts over. The chains holding me squeak as I sway, rutting a groove in the dirt beneath me. With the heel of my sneakers I dig up a child's barrette. My throat clogs.

I'm sitting on a swing, recalling how he sat here, too. He soared high above the ground, shrieking.

A little while ago an elderly woman was pulling weeds behind the slide.

"Where are you from?" she asked me in Japanese.

"America." I said it with pride, in that don't-you-wish-you-could-be-so-lucky tone.

"*Ah, so.*" She nodded. The skin around her eyes crinkled, but her smile was stiff. She seemed to be reflecting, remembering, and she turned away.

Maybe she'd heard about me.

Now I'm alone, swinging, smoking a cigarette. A few years ago I would never have lit up in public. I kept up appearances. I hid my liquor bottles in the depths of the trash container. Actually, I didn't drink much at all then. I intended to be beyond reproach.

A crow lands on the telephone wire and looks down at me, caws. Even the birds are scolding me. More crows come, and they start jabbering with each other, and I am forgotten.

Finally, the hour arrives. The hour of soldier-suited children lugging red satchels, kicking at rocks and cans as they go along. They pass in groups of three or four, sometimes bumping each other and laughing. Usually there is one serious older child leading the way. Sometimes a mother.

I stub out my cigarette in the sand. I bury it deep, pat the dirt over it. I shade my eyes against the mid-afternoon glare, look down the lane.

Even from a distance I know exactly which one is him. He is with two other boys, but he scuffles along, chin to chest, ignoring the others. His yellow hat is wadded into his jacket pocket. The brass buttons of his blazer catch the sun. He is coming this way.

I rise from the swing, heart pounding. I walk to the edge of the playground. A quartet of pony-tailed girls crosses to the other side of the road when they see me. They giggle behind their little hands and when they are just beyond me, safe, they begin to recite all of the English phrases they know: "Hello," "my name is..." (which they say as "mayonnaise," the mispronunciation a popular joke among schoolchildren), "thank you very much." San kyu berry muchi.

I barely hear them. He is coming closer, but he hasn't looked up yet. I see that his dark brown hair is longer than before, brushing over his ears. He is deeply tanned from outdoor play. An adhesive bandage is pasted over his left knee.

One of his friends grabs the yellow hat from his pocket and tosses it into the air.

"*Oi,*" he says, irritated. "*Kaeshite.*" Give it back. He swipes at the boy's head.

The other two boys toss the hat back and forth, but I can tell from their high, excited voices, from the way that they keep in line, that they are teasing him out of affection. They are not bullies, not the little monsters who steal lunch money and wield knives that you read about in the newspaper. They are only trying to pull him out of himself, to bring his attention to them.

I am so caught up in watching them that I almost forget why I am here. Remembering, I raise my hand as far as my temple and call out, "Kei!"

He looks up, searches for a moment, and finds me.

From this close I can see the lush fringe of his lashes, the dimples in his cheeks. In his eyes, I detect yearning. Just for a moment. Because then, out of nowhere, his grandmother appears. She must have seen me. She must have noticed me even as I stood entranced by this boy. She runs to him and the others fall away.

"Kei!" I shout again, but she won't let him look at me.

She holds his head firmly against her side and rushes him off down the street and I can do nothing but watch.

I have lost him again. I have lost my son Kei.

# 1989

I CAME TO JAPAN BECAUSE A MAN HAD BROKEN MY HEART. FOR YEARS, I had been dreaming of Africa. My bookshelves were crammed with stories of the savanna, of women flying planes over herds of elephants, of Karen Blixen farming coffee on her plantation, of spinster schoolteachers getting it on with white hunters. I'd thought that I'd become a wildlife photographer for National Geographic, or maybe open a gallery of African art. Or maybe I'd write some stories myself. I'd been accepted into the Peace Corps. My posting was Cameroon. But Philip went to Africa before I did. Dakar, Senegal, to be exact. He'd already made his plans by the time I'd met him. When we broke up, I knew that going to Africa myself would fuel my hope. I would always be waiting, expecting to run into him, the way I'd once encountered a long-ago neighbor at the coat check of the Louvre. My eyes would follow every khaki-clad pair of legs up to the face that might be his. I'd be haunting ex-pat bars and embassy parties in search of him. And so when my brother suggested a fellowship for artists in Japan, I saw my chance to make a clean break.

• • • • •

As soon as I knew I'd be going to Japan, I began to study the language. I picked up a few textbooks from the university bookstore, put up an ad (soon answered by a Junji Shimada) and set myself the task of learning one Chinese character a day. That is, after I'd spent a week mastering two phonetic alphabets—*hiragana*, for Japanese words, and *katakana*, for the lingo borrowed from abroad.

"You don't have to go all the way to Japan to forget about him," my mother said when I first told her of my plans. "And besides he might come back to you. After Africa."

Strange words from the woman who'd walked out on her husband, my father, because he didn't deserve her and who'd pretty much given up on men after that.

But then again, she'd been Philip's number one fan. Early on in our relationship, he'd invited himself to her house for Thanksgiving dinner. That year my brothers were going to hang out with our father and his new wife at a timeshare on the coast. They had already chartered a boat for deep sea fishing, something that didn't interest me in the least. Besides, I wasn't about to abandon our mother and her twenty-five pound turkey.

Philip showed up with a bouquet of flowers ("Freesias! My favorite!"), a bottle of Beaujolais, and a Nina Simone album. I'd told him how my mother loved Nina Simone.

That evening after he'd gone home, we had a few glasses of wine together and my mother said, "Not just any guy would be willing to come to your house for a major holiday a month into the relationship."

I nodded and sipped from my glass. "He also volunteered to be my date for Katie's wedding."

Katie McGraw was my oldest friend and I was going to be the maid of honor. Philip would have to sit by himself during the ceremony.

"Obviously he's serious about you." She gave me a pat on the knee and hauled herself off to bed.

I appreciated that in spite of my dad and his infidelities she was still encouraging me to fall in love. She offered me the possibility of happily-ever-after and that was like a gift. At least that's how I felt then.

By the time I boarded the plane in Atlanta, leaving my mother at the gate, I was ready to forget all about falling in love. I wanted to lose myself in another language. After all that cramming, I was confident that I'd be able to order a bowl of noodles once I got to Narita. And I could probably make it clear to a cab driver that I wanted to go to the Keio Plaza in Shinjuku, where my room was reserved.

I stashed my textbooks in the overhead bin and ordered a glass of wine.

Soon I would be in a place where no one knew anything about me, where I would be free to reconstruct my life. Without Philip.

I'd told the interview panel that I was following in the footsteps of Blondelle Malone, a woman painter who'd lived just a few blocks from the house where I grew up, albeit a hundred years earlier.

When I was twelve, I'd checked her biography out of the public library and never returned it. Imagining her life and her lost paintings was enough to intrigue me. Although her biographer tended toward condescension, I thought that maybe she'd been wrong. Maybe Blondelle had been a victim of the times—a woman, when men held the power; an Impressionist, when the fashion was fauve. For all I knew, she had been a great, forgotten artist, in the same way that Frida Kahlo had been. Slagged, and then resurrected. But where were her paintings? I amused myself by thinking I'd solve this great mystery. And if I couldn't find them, I'd just paint them again. I'd replace them, as it were.

• • • • •

In Tokyo, I lugged my bags to the curb and hailed a taxi. The yellow vehicle pulled up in front of me and the back passenger door opened as if by magic. The driver, a gnomish man with white-gloved hands, lifted my three suitcases with surprising ease and stashed them in the trunk. I slid onto the seat of the car and laid my head back against the lace antimacassar. A box of tissues encased in ruffled cloth sat under the back window like a bakery cake.

"Okay," the driver said, taking his place at the wheel. "Where you wanna go?"

I impressed him with a stream of Japanese.

He grunted with grudging respect, and then guided the car into traffic.

I didn't want to talk just then. I hoped he wouldn't be one of those chatty drivers. He wasn't. At the stoplights, he studied me via rearview mirror, a slight frown on his face. Otherwise, he seemed intent on the high school baseball game blaring from his car radio.

The city outside my window was clean. Pure. Whitewashed buildings, devoid of graffiti. The streets were free of trash. The cars that traveled upon them seemed to be recent models, and washed that day. I didn't see a single dent.

The inside of the taxi smelled of pomade and faded tobacco. An air freshener was affixed to the dash. I spent a moment concentrating on these smells, wanting to save them. I tried to memorize the buildings (not sky high as in New York, for instance; there were earthquakes here), the billboards pushing Coca Cola and some drink called Pocari Sweat. The sight of Mt. Fuji, hazy in the distance.

I loved the perfect manners of the hotel staff. The attendant bowed as he ushered me into the elevator. The other young man who pushed my suitcases on a trolley refused my offer of a tip and backed away, smiling.

I loved the crisp white sheets of my bed, and the tea set laid out with rice crackers wrapped in paper that resembled kimono fabric.

Exhaustion surged and threatened to pull me under, but I wanted to see, hear, touch, smell, taste, do more. I brewed a cup of green tea and crunched a cracker. Then I flicked on the television. A newscast was about to begin. The announcers bowed in unison before reading the news. My first day in Japan. My new life.

• • • • •

The next morning, over a bowl of room service miso soup, I cracked open a guidebook and plotted my day. I'd start out with a visit to the Tokyo National Museum in Ueno Park, then drop by the zoo to see the panda (I'd never seen one in person). After that I'd take the subway to Shinjuku and have lunch at one of the stand-up noodle bars I'd heard about. I expected the crowds and the neon and the video screens would wear me out, so as my last outing of the day, I'd visit a temple for a bit of serenity.

At Ueno Zoo, I went straight for Ling Ling. A group of small children in uniform crowded in front of the display, pressing their noses against glass. "Panda-san!" they called. "Panda-san!" One little boy pounded the window with his fist, earning a mild reproach from a young woman who was probably his teacher.

Over the yellow-capped heads, I could see Ling Ling crouched in a corner. The concrete floor was strewn with a few stalks of limp bamboo. The animal had no companions, and I wondered if she remembered China, her mother, others of her kind.

A camera flashed nearby and I turned away.

At the temple, I trailed a tour group—a bunch of sixtyish women in their holiday best, with a few men tagging along. They laughed loudly, slapping each other as they picked their way along the stone path. Off to my left, a group of junior high school students was stepping onto risers, preparing for a commemorative photo.

I'd been stupid to expect peace. This was a major tourist attraction. If I wanted to meditate, I'd have to find some mountain monastery. I took to people-watching instead. I tried to guess who was from the city, and who was from the country. I didn't expect to see any other foreigners, but then I did.

It was a man. The exact size and shape of Philip. I thought I remembered those khaki trousers, that Hard Rock Café T-shirt.

The light was in my eyes, so his face was obscured by a flash of brilliance.

I pulled my jacket collar around my face and tried to retract my head like a turtle. I wanted to be seen, and I didn't.

He was coming toward me, a Japanese girl, a sprig of a woman, latched onto his arm. He lied to me, I thought. He didn't go to Africa at all. He's here in Japan. The fat noodles I'd consumed earlier threatened to come back up. I felt so dizzy, I had to sit down right there on the walkway.

"Are you alright?" Suddenly he was standing above me, concern filling his eyes. Not Philip's eyes.

I let him pull me to my feet. It wasn't Philip. His hair was a little darker, I now saw. He was older by maybe a decade. His companion studied me with wide-open eyes.

"I'm so embarrassed," I said, brushing a leaf from the seat of my pants. "My head just started spinning all of a sudden. Must be jet lag."

"Are you pregnant?" the woman asked.

The man shot her a look, but I just laughed. "No. No chance of that."

"Why don't you join us for a cup of coffee or something?" the man said. "Maybe you need to sit down for awhile."

I followed them to a little tea house and let the woman order for me, although I could have done it myself. The man didn't seem to speak Japanese.

"How long have you been here?" I asked him.

"Three years." He ducked his head. "I know, I know. My Japanese should be better, but it's so easy to get by without it. You've got English-language newspapers and magazines. TV's bilingual. And there are so many foreigners here."

"Hmmm." I stirred creamer into my individually brewed cup of coffee. "So is it like that everywhere?"

He shrugged. "I went cycling in Tokushima—that's in Shikoku—over the Bon holidays and nobody speaks English down there. I didn't run into a single American."

19

"Is that so?"

When I got back to my hotel room, I pulled out a map and a train schedule. In the morning, I would go to Tokushima.

• • • • •

I took one train and then another till I got to Tokushima City, and then I changed trains again and went all the way to the southern coast. I got off in a little seaside town that smelled of fish and kelp and asked for directions to the nearest hotel.

In Tokyo, no one had looked at me, but the middle-aged woman at the front desk dropped her pen when I walked in. "*Sumimasen, sumimasen.*"

"No, *I'm* sorry," I said in Japanese. "Do you have any rooms available?"

She laughed and put a hand to her chest. "Oh, you speak Japanese. I am relieved."

I laughed along with her and followed her to my room.

She told me that she had never rented a room to a foreigner before.

"So you don't get too many tourists from abroad?"

"No, no."

I nodded, satisfied. This was just the place I'd been looking for.

"There's just Eric," she said.

I froze. "Eric? He's what? American?"

"Yes, American. Very handsome." She told me that he'd been around for a couple of years, having spent two years already in Tokyo as a male model. He taught English conversation at Happy English School, a private enterprise in a room upstairs from a yakitori shop. "Do you want me to introduce you?"

"No, thanks," I said. If I stuck around, I figured I'd run into him soon enough.

A couple days later, the hotel lady directed me to a real estate agent. By the end of the week, I'd rented an apartment and furnished it with cushions and a table.

I spent the following days wandering around the town. I found a little bakery that made pain au chocolat, and the post office from which you could have sweet potatoes sent to any part of Japan. After three days, I found the café that made the best cup of Jamaican Blue Mountain coffee, and a bookstore that stocked the *Japan Times*.

• • • • •

I saw Eric for the first time after a night of insomnia. I took my sketchpad down to the cove, along with a thermos of hot coffee and some rice balls wrapped in dried seaweed and sat on the beach. I was always hoping for visions of dolphins or whales breeching, but so far I'd seen only waves and half a dozen early morning surfers.

I'd never learned to surf, although I'd known surfers all my life. My brothers, for instance. At sixteen, when they were jockeys of the cerulean waves, I had a longing for another kind of blue, a deep velvet midnight blue, the color that goes well with stars and bourbon, that hangs a dark veil over Gatsby-esque parties, or that complements a scene of a rowboat drifting on a northern lake at night. Maybe there was an escaped boy in the boat, floating away from home so that he can smoke one of his daddy's cigarettes without getting caught (as if Mama wouldn't smell it on his indigo jean jacket) or maybe a broken-hearted teen-aged girl contemplating a swan dive to the muck at the bottom of the lake with an anchor or rocks, a la Virginia Woolf. Or maybe lovers trying to figure out the mysteries of the body with their backs against planks, splinters working their way into moon-pale flesh under that dark blue sky. But I preferred the empty rowboat. Unmoored. Just drifting. There was a story there. Characters. Who forgot to tie the boat to shore? Whose boat was it? And what would happen when its owner discovered its loss? This was a story that I could paint.

On the beach that morning, I was looking for another tale to tell. And then, I caught sight of a figure gliding on the surf, his broad upper body backlit by sunrise. His balance was perfect. I thought of Neptune and I wondered why he wasn't holding a forked spear.

The wave subsided. The ride over, he jumped off the board, brought it under his arm, and came onto shore.

He thought he was alone. He shook his head like a rain-drenched dog, and began to peel off his navy wetsuit. I was afraid that he was going to strip right there.

"Hey," I shouted. "Good morning."

He stopped in mid-motion, his chest bared. "Oh. Hi." Then he loped over to me. "You must be Jill."

He had the bluest eyes I'd ever seen. They disappeared into crinkles when he smiled. "Single American woman who looks like Andie McDowell and likes to draw pictures."

"Andie McDowell? Huh."

I offered him some of my coffee. I didn't have an extra cup, so we sipped from the same plastic mug, just as I'd learned Japanese bride and groom share a cup during their wedding. I don't know why I thought of marriage. I'd already ascertained that this Eric was a bit of a playboy, and although I was impressed by his washboard stomach, his solid shoulders and toothy smile, I didn't think he was my type. There were foreign men who stayed in Japan just to be adored by the native women.

Japanese women tended to believe that American men were like the romantic heroes they'd seen in Hollywood movies. They were used to walking behind men who grunted responses, who wouldn't hold open doors, who didn't send flowers. On Valentine's Day, I'd heard, Japanese women gave their men chocolate and got nothing in return. Even the most ordinary of Western men rivaled Prince Charming next to that.

As if to confirm my assumption, a slim young woman with about two feet of straight black hair ambled onto the beach. A wetsuit was pasted to her boyish figure. She lugged a boogie board under one arm.

Eric raised his hand and waved. "Akemi! Over here!"

"Early morning date, huh?"

He shrugged. "I work afternoons and nights. She works all day."

I wondered if they had planned to have sex on the beach. And then I remembered sitting on another beach on the other side of the world, my elbows sunk in the sand, the day Philip told me he no longer loved me.

"Well, I'd better be off," I said.

"Hey, what were you drawing anyway?"

I didn't want to show him my sketch of a surfer. I figured it would go to his head. "Nothing. I was just doodling." I closed my pad and screwed the lid on my thermos. Then I stood up and brushed the sand off my legs and bottom.

When I reached the edge of the beach, I turned and looked back. Eric and Akemi were kissing, their thinly clad bodies pressed tightly together. I watched a little longer before I had to close my eyes.

• • • • •

On another morning a couple of weeks later, I walked down to the beach again.

Eric was there, sitting in the sand, playing a banjo. The tune he was plucking sounded like half of "Dueling Banjos" from the movie *Deliverance*. When he saw me, he started playing faster. At the end of the song, his hand flew away from the strings and he threw back his head. Song over, he turned to me with perfect composure and said, "Good morning. I was just thinking about you."

I dropped down beside him. "Were you?"

"Yeah. My next-door neighbor runs a snack and she's looking for some foreign talent, as it were. She's a good person. She looks out for her girls. Anyway, I thought you might be interested."

"Are you talking about hostessing?" I'd heard about the bars where women were paid to pour drinks and flirt.

"She's got a couple of Filipinas, but she'd love to have an

American on staff. It's not a bad place—no yakuza. And you don't have to dress up in a kinky sailor girl costume or whatever."

I was silent for a moment, watching the waves crest and fall.

"It's easy money," he went on. "You could make a hundred bucks in a night. Under the table."

I let the idea enter my mind. I wasn't hard up for cash, but I'd been bored recently and a bit lonely. I could work at this place a few weeks, accumulate some anecdotes, and improve my Japanese.

"Why are you so gung ho?" I asked. "Do you have an investment in the place?"

Eric shrugged. "I'm just trying to help you both out."

"All right," I shrugged back. "Introduce me to her. I'll give it some thought."

We made arrangements to meet at the Cha Cha Club the following afternoon.

I toyed with the idea of cleavage and eye shadow. I figured Mama Morita would expect her hostesses to be tarted up a bit. But then I decided to go to the meeting in the jeans and oversized button-down shirt that I was already wearing. I didn't want to appear too eager. It's not as if I was dying to take the job.

I was glad to see Eric in surfer shorts and a T-shirt. He stood beneath the club's sign. Paint was flaking from the door. The place was wedged between a bakery and a bookstore stocked mainly with manga, the thick pulpy comic books that were so popular. There were no windows to the Cha Cha Club, only that door with its peeling white paint and a heavy brass knocker.

"Ready?" Eric asked.

I nodded.

He tried the handle and, finding it unlocked, pushed into the dim interior of the club. Even in muted lighting, the place looked shabby. The upholstered chairs were saggy and fading. A poster featuring a bare-breasted woman curled at the corners. Mama Morita, with her blood red lipstick and bottle-blond hair, was the brightest thing in the room. She stepped from behind the bar and held out her hand to me. Her nails appeared to be freshly polished. "How do you do?" she said. "Nice to meet you."

Out of the corner of my eye, I saw Eric wink at her. I wondered if he'd coached her in English.

She nodded to one of the low sofas and we all sat down.

"Whiskey?" she asked.

It seemed a bit early in the day for the hard stuff. I'd seen train travelers cracking open cans of sake at eight a.m., but I didn't usually start drinking till dusk. "A glass of water would be fine."

The rest of the interview was conducted in Japanese, Mama Morita having presumably exhausted her English vocabulary. She didn't ask me about previous work experience or even why I thought I wanted the job. I'd expected that she'd ask me to audition. After all, hostesses were often called upon to join in the karaoke and my main role would be as entertainer. I would have to banter.

Mama Morita wanted to know the things that every other person I'd met in Japan had asked me. What was I doing there? How did I choose this downtrodden seaside village as opposed to some glittering city? And wasn't my mother beside herself with worry and loneliness with me, her daughter, so far away?

Mama Morita had a daughter herself, she confided. She was going to college, but sometimes came to help out at the club. Mama Morita had never married the girl's father, but he'd been kind enough to give her his name. Just as he'd been kind enough to set her mother up with this snack. He probably had a wife and other children besides. I wondered how they felt about this woman in the white silk pantsuit and flashing jewelry. Did they know anything about her at all?

"So?" Eric said, when my glass of water had been refilled for the third time. Talk had wound down to clucks and sighs. "When do you want to start?"

I was surprised. I'd assumed that she'd call in a day or two or send word through Eric.

I looked at the shelves laden with bottles of Johnny Walker and Jack Daniels. I saw myself in the mirror behind the bar looking gaunt and pale. "Tonight?"

Mama Morita nodded. "Tonight," she repeated. "Eight o'clock."

She reached out her hand and we shook. Eric grabbed a last handful of peanuts from the cut-glass bowl on the table and we rose to leave.

As Mama Morita ushered us to the door, she murmured something to Eric.

"What did she say?" I asked once we were out on the sidewalk, assailed by the blinding rays of the late afternoon sun.

"She told me to tell you to wear a dress."

• • • • •

Here is what I remember from my first night: pomade and smoke-burned eyes, and vomit in my lap (rare, according to Mama Morita, but it happens), and the drone of a particularly poor singer, who sometimes took his turn at karaoke. I was wearing new shoes that pinched my toes together and I'd forgotten to wear a slip between my silk skirt and pantyhose, so the fabric clung to my legs. I drank too much *mizuwari*, trying to be a good sport about the whole thing, till Mama Morita took me aside and clued me in on the bucket placed under the table for discreet disposal of drinks.

And then the next day, I woke to the sunlight crashing through the window, make-up smeared on my pillow and a rotten taste in my mouth. I'd fallen into bed as soon as I'd gotten home at three a.m., not bothering to brush my teeth. My smoky skirt and blouse were crumpled next to the bed.

I wanted to crawl back into the night and sleep, but then the phone jangled and I had to answer it just so the ringing would stop hurting my head.

It was Eric.

"So?"

26

"So what?"

"How'd it go?"

And so I told him as much as I remembered. I hadn't found my groove yet, I said, but I'd give it another try. I knew he was calling on behalf of my new employer. When he'd gotten the information that he needed, that I would continue working at the Cha Cha Club, he released me, and I slept through the best light of the day.

• • • • •

It got better after that. I liked the other women who worked there. I found their sassy no-nonsense approach to life refreshing after the constant pageant of manners that went on in the world outside. Sometimes it was even fun to flirt with the men, most of them married, who frequented the place. And it was easy. Drunk men will laugh at the lamest of jokes.

One evening we hostesses were sitting around drinking cold barley tea. The place hadn't opened for business yet. We were just getting set up.

Mama Morita looked at me and said, "Eric say you artist."

I nodded slowly, took a sip of tea. "Yes, I paint."

"You paint picture for that wall," she said pointing to the poster of the bare-breasted woman.

I thought that I'd be happy not to have those nipples staring at me all the time, but I couldn't imagine what kind of image she'd want in its place.

"Do you want something erotic?" I asked. "*Echi* picture?"

"No, no, no." Mama Morita waved her hand back and forth as if to warn me against danger. "Paint what you like. I give you money."

Thus, my first commission.

• • • • •

Whenever I took to the streets, I brought my camera and sketchbook along. I'd be stopped in my tracks by a figure jutting from the corner of a roof—a fish or a demon-like creature meant to ward off harm. I liked the latched gates that suggested hidden gardens and secret lives. I took a lot of pictures of schoolchildren in matching sailor-collared jackets and jaunty hats just because they began posing at the sight of the camera slung over my shoulder.

I had no idea of what to paint for Mama Morita.

And then there was a typhoon. Eric called to warn me about it.

"Batten down the hatches," he said. "Number 7 is on its way."

"Number 7?"

"Yeah, in Japan they're numbered. No cute names for these babies."

I decided to name the approaching storm myself: Typhoon Francesca. From what I could make out on TV, she was swirling around Kyushu. She was due in our little town the following morning.

It was my first typhoon and I didn't know what to expect. I'd heard stories about the legendary typhoon of thirty years back. Houses had flooded, photo albums and chairs and sacks of rice had washed away. People had drowned and washed ashore days later with seaweed in their hair.

A month before, Hurricane Hugo had razed the Carolina coast. Eight-bedroom beach houses had been swept from their stilts, boats impaled on palmetto trees. I wondered if anything had happened to the house in North Myrtle Beach where Philip had spent the summer. I half-hoped that it was gone—a memory resting on the bottom of the ocean.

I tied my washing machine to the railing of the verandah and tacked flattened cardboard boxes over the windows. Neighbors were busy shuttering their own windows and sliding glass doors.

The sky was still blue just before sunset, but the wind was beginning to whisper messages from afar. Hair whipped into my face when I stepped outside for one last look. Then I took a bath, prepared candles, and went to bed.

When I woke up, I thought a freight train was bearing down on my apartment building. I could feel the concrete sway and shiver. Francesca was a big bad wolf, trying to blow my house down. I flicked the light switch, testing. The room became bright. Everything was still working, so I made coffee and heated a croissant in my toaster oven. Every rattle of the door made my heart beat a little faster.

It was like that for two or three hours, and then the wind died down. All I could hear was rain. The cardboard was flapping at the window, duct tape having been no match for Typhoon Francesa. I went outside and tore it down. The clouds were well on their way east.

By afternoon, the sun was out, so I decided to go for a walk. I picked my way through fallen branches, a roof tile or two, a child's plastic bucket. All of the houses were still standing, as far as I could tell. Some people were out raking up their yards or sweeping off steps.

I went all the way to the beach. The immense waves were the last reminder of the ferocious storm that had passed through. A dozen or so surfers were out riding the waters. I stood watching them for awhile.

The sand was littered with driftwood and debris. There were rusty old cans, pieces of furniture, chunks of boats. Even so, there was something magnificent about the scene—the angry waves, their frothy wake, the cliffs towering over the cove and the surfers themselves.

I saw three young men emerge from the sea. They wore black wetsuits trimmed in neon colors—yellow, pink, and green. Their muscles stood out in relief against the shiny material and I thought they looked like comic book Superheroes. They seemed exhausted, yet also invigorated.

I lifted my camera and peered through the viewfinder. This was it.

This was the picture that I would paint for Mama Morita. Excitement made me snap faster. By the time the surfers had made their way up the beach, I had shot an entire role of film.

After they'd left, I dropped down on the sand and began sketching. In another day, I would begin to paint.

• • • • •

I got an invitation in the mail to a gallery opening at the prefectural museum. I'd never heard of the artist, Yamashita Kikuji, but I thought I would go all the same. On that Friday afternoon, I donned a simple black dress and complicated jewelry I'd made myself from beads and wire, and boarded a bus. The Culture Forest, a collection of cultural facilities, was on the edge of Tokushima City, at the base of a mountain. A creek ran along the road leading to the museum and there were some men casting their lines into the slow-moving water. Herons waded in the shallows. I thought that the scene might be something to put on canvas.

The bus stopped in front of a huge fountain spewing water twelve feet into the air. I got off and made my way to the museum.

I'd been to a few gallery shows in South Carolina. One was of a series of oil paintings of chickens. Tongue-searing chili had been served. Visitors had slouched around with plastic bowls, making squawking noises.

This show was something else. I wandered into a throng of chatty old men, some of them with berets, the mark of a Japanese bohemian, and shoulder-length white hair. There were only a couple of women, and one man in a black leather jacket who looked to be a few years older than me. He had a neatly clipped beard, which was just as unconventional as the white hair on the elderly gentlemen.

Somewhere a clock bonged the hour and the murmurings died down. The curator, dressed as if for mourning in a black suit and tie, stepped up to a microphone and made a standard greeting—something about weather and how everyone was so good to turn out in spite of their general busyness. And then he rambled on a bit about Yamashita Kikuji, who, I gathered from my limited Japanese, had been born in Tokushima Prefecture, and had died.

Then he introduced one of the women who was dressed in a drab-colored kimono. She was the widow of the artist whose work we had all come to see.

I wondered what kind of role she had played in her husband's life. Had she sat for him in the nude or just served his tea? Her deep bows and the hands layered so demurely at her waist suggested servitude. But in Japan, appearances can be deceptive. I preferred to imagine her as a young woman with her black hair unpinned and falling to her waist, her own brush flying over canvas.

When she had finished speaking, she motioned toward the gallery entrance, and the old men, perhaps long ago schoolmates of the deceased painter, began to flow toward the exhibit.

I admit I did not know much about contemporary Japanese art. I had books of woodblock prints by Hokusai and Utamaro, pictures of the water trade and images of Mt. Fuji, but I had never seen the likes of Yamashita's paintings. The images hung on the white walls were by turns grotesque and surreal. A woman with a geisha's face but wearing blood-spattered pajamas instead of kimono sat in a chair. Headless soldiers hovered behind her. In another painting, bunraku puppets looked down upon an old couple sitting around their brazier while a young boy in school uniform rode a hawk among bubbles.

"He killed during the war," a voice said behind me. "And after that, he painted his remorse."

I turned to see the guy with the beard. He was only a few inches taller than I was. I thought that his leather jacket would fit me quite well. I inhaled his scent of soap and cigarettes and mint chewing gum.

"You speak English," I said. His accent was surprisingly natural.

"Yes. I lived in San Francisco for awhile. When I was a student."

"And you are interested in art," I said.

"And so are you." He held out his hand. I noticed his fingernails were manicured. "I'm Yusuke Yamashiro."

"Jill Parker. Nice to meet you."

He looked at me as if he were trying to memorize my face. I wasn't used to such scrutiny. I felt suddenly shy, but I held his gaze, looked back into his big, rounded eyes. There were a few single men living in my apartment building, but they ducked their heads when they saw me and didn't respond to my greetings. This man, however, was clearly not afraid of me. He'd lived in the States after all. He'd probably dated American women.

We wandered through the rest of the exhibit together, Yusuke providing commentary. From time to time, he put his hand on the small of my back, guiding me. I liked feeling the heat of his fingers there. I let my arm brush against his. Afterward, he invited me to join him for coffee and I accepted.

When Yusuke asked me why I'd come to Japan, I told him that it was because of Blondelle Malone. Blondelle and I had both come of age painting gardens in South Carolina, though she'd been born in the 1800s. She left Columbia to scour the world for inspiration for her art. I lived in her old neighborhood and I liked to walk past her former house and imagine her on that slow ship sailing for Yokohama. I thought that I would one day, too, sit in the shadow of Mt. Fuji with my easel and big picture hat and paint all that I saw. Children would bring me daffodils and branches of cherry blossom trees, just as they did to her. And men would beg to marry me, but I would decline in the name of my continuing commitment to art.

"Do you still feel that way?" Yusuke asked. He sat in the booth across from me, his arm draped over the banquette. His teeth, I must say, were perfect. "About marriage, I mean."

"Not really," I said. "I think I'd like to get married some day."

He stared at me for a moment, then dropped a sugar cube into his coffee and stirred. "I'd like to see some of your paintings. I run a small gallery. Maybe I could help you out."

I didn't have anywhere near enough work for an exhibition, but I thought that I might have one or two paintings that were good enough for a group show. At any rate, I wasn't about to pass on what seemed to be a golden opportunity. "Sure. When?"

"How about tomorrow evening?"

I'd promised Mama Morita that I'd fill in for one her girls. I didn't think that I could back out. "Uh, tomorrow's not good."

"Do you have a date?" His eyes twinkled.

"No, no. I'm working."

"You're an English teacher?"

I didn't really want to tell him that I was moonlighting as a snack hostess. I knew that some men looked down on women in the water trade and I didn't want him to think that I was loose. But I also felt compelled to be honest with him and I hoped that his time in America had made a liberal out of him. So I told him about the Cha Cha Club.

I thought I saw his eyebrows draw together in a frown, but when he looked up at me again, he was smiling. "How about the day after?"

"That would be great."

• • • • •

Usually Thursdays were a little slow at the Cha Cha Club, but that week, we had a customer in every available seat.

Mama Morita assigned Veronica, a beautiful Filipina with gazelle eyes and boyish hips, and me to a table of businessmen who worked at an international pharmaceutical company. They had already loosened their ties. They'd obviously been drinking before they reached our tattered sofas.

One guy appeared to be the ringleader. Maybe he was their boss. Anyhow, he called for the bottle of Jack Daniels that he kept behind the bar and Mama Morita brought it out on a lacquered tray. Veronica poured the drinks while I lit cigarettes. Then the guy barked out for the songbook, and Mama Morita hurried over and presented it to him, even though it had been sitting on the table, right under his nose.

We were so busy, that it took me a few minutes to notice the somber man sitting right next to me. He didn't smoke and he took only one sip of his drink and then left it on the table, watching the ice cubes melt.

"Peanuts?" I held the dish within plucking distance. I felt a little guilty. My job was to entertain him, but he seemed so morose.

"No, thank you," he said in English. "I have no appetite."

His cronies seemed to be leaving him alone. Maybe they knew what his deal was already. At any rate, they were busily picking out their numbers for karaoke.

"Not too thrilled to be here, are you?" I asked.

He didn't understand my English, so I tried to rephrase it in bungled Japanese.

"Today is my daughter's birthday," he said, cutting me off. He was still staring at his drink.

"Oh." I wasn't sure why this would make him so sad. "I guess you wanted to spend this evening with your little girl, huh?"

"Yes, of course," he said. "But it's impossible."

It was only nine o'clock. "Oh, well, you could go home right now," I said. "I won't tell. And your buddies are so wasted right now that they probably wouldn't even notice."

We both observed the other three men in the group for a moment. Their faces were blazing red, their eyes mere slits. One of them was trying to nuzzle Veronica, but she kept pushing him away. She was surprisingly strong for having such a stick figure.

"You don't understand," the man said. "My daughter lives with my ex-wife. She thinks that I am dead."

"Why would she think that?"

"Because my wife told her so. She wanted to start her life all over again as if I didn't exist."

I tried to absorb this, but I'd already had a couple of shots of whiskey myself. "Don't you have visitation rights? Can't you see her on week-ends and school holidays at least?"

He snorted. "Yeah, yeah. I've seen your Hollywood movies.

This is not U.S.A. where everyone gets a divorce and then stays best friends. There is no joint custody here. There is divorce and then mothers poison their children's minds against the fathers who worked so hard to take care of them."

"I'm sorry," I said quietly. "Maybe you should have a drink."

He reached into his inner jacket pocket then and pulled out a photo. It was creased and a little wilted from having been handled so much. But the face of the little girl was clear. Her head was cocked to one side, and her smile revealed a gap where she had lost a tooth. Pigtails sprouted from the sides of her head.

"She's beautiful," I said, although I thought she was merely an ordinary-looking child.

He gave me a grim nod and then he put the photo back in his pocket, stood up, and left the club as I had suggested.

One of the other men was engaged in singing about a tryst at a riverside hotel. His cohorts were clapping in time. They took no notice of the other man's leaving.

I sat there for a few minutes wondering if I had somehow failed as a hostess. Then I shook my head a little as if just that movement could expel all dark thoughts, and began clapping with the others. I poured whiskey over ice for one man, lit another's cigarette, brushed a hand off of my knee.

Out of the corner of my eye, I saw the door open and a solitary figure walk in. He seemed hesitant—not one of our usual customers. I turned and looked. And then I blushed.

Yusuke was standing there by the bar, chatting with Mama Morita. He looked splendid in a checked raw silk jacket and khaki pants—a nice antidote to all of the navy polyester I saw every night. He made the Cha Cha Club appear one degree more shabby than it already was.

Mama Morita nodded her head and gestured in my direction.

Even though I was embarrassed, I knew that she would be glad I'd brought in a customer. I felt a little proud.

There was really no place to sit, so she pulled a couple of

chairs aside for us, offered us the corner of someone else's glass-topped table.

"So," I said. "You found me."

"Nice place," he said, nodding to the room.

I couldn't tell if he was being sarcastic. His tone was pleasant enough, but I wasn't sure.

"That's my painting," I said, pointing to the surfers on the wall. I wanted to get that out before he had a chance to make some withering comment.

He studied the three men in wet suits emerging from a ravaged landscape. They were faceless, like Japanese ghosts.

"Nice," Yusuke said. "How did your work wind up in this place?"

I explained to him about my commission. Mama Morita had paid me fifty thousand yen for the canvas. It was enough for one month's rent. She had hinted that she might ask for another. A birthday present for her daughter, maybe. Something for her living room at home.

"You could have gotten more for it," he said. "At least twice that."

He might have been right. This was during the bubble years when businessmen laid out small fortunes for works by Van Gogh and Monet. Art had cachet then. And people had money to burn. I saw it flowing between hands every night, as the foreign liquor was poured until dawn.

"You know, you don't have to work here," he said. "If you can paint like that, you owe it to yourself to quit."

It never occurred to me that he might have had ulterior motives, that the idea of courting a hostess was unsavory to him. I was stuck on the vision of myself he presented to me. I thought that maybe I was a better artist than I'd ever thought I could be.

I moved a little bit closer to him and our knees touched.

He looked at me for a moment, then drew his legs aside. "I'll see you tomorrow," he said, standing.

As I watched him take out his wallet and prepare to leave, I felt oddly rebuffed. He hadn't touched his drink, hadn't touched me. My hostess skills were going down the drain.

# 1997

IT IS EVENING, HOURS AFTER I'VE SAT IN THE PARK, WATCHING MY SON.
I am at the table with a bowl of cream stew, thinking about Kei.
I'm already dressed for work, in a black silk ensemble that I wore
two nights ago and haven't yet washed. It still smells of cigarettes,
even though I aired it out on the balcony. The label reads "Dry
Clean Only," but I'd rather not waste the money. Tomorrow I'll
try washing it in the sink. I'm eating my cream stew, thinking
about the way the sunlight ignited Kei's hair, the ginger strands,
when the doorbell rings.

I never answer the door unless I am expecting company. Most
of the time, I don't even bother to glance through the peep-
hole. We get a lot of door-to-door salespeople in this apartment
complex. They peddle everything from bras to strawberries. And
I, the fallen foreigner, get a good number of visits from cruel-
hearted children. They come to pester and gawk. They stuff used
tissues and wads of chewed gum through my mail slot. Once, a
dead bird.

The doorbell chimes again and again. I count up to ten, and
then I plug my ears with my fingers. Eric would call out my name.
I know it isn't him anyway; this is the hour of his yoga class. He
is not leaning on my doorbell, but bending and stretching with
Japanese housewives.

Now there is pounding. The door vibrates. I hear the scuffle of feet and then a phlegmy cough and I know that it is some man and that he is after me.

I think of turning off the lights, but that would give me away. I hold my breath until the pounding stops and the footsteps click down the corridor. I listen to the elevator doors sliding open and closed, the labored grind of machinery as my visitor is lowered to the first floor. A car door, opening and slamming. The rev of a souped-up engine.

I've lost my appetite. I dump my cream stew, the bits of carrots and pork, into the trash and brush my teeth; put on lipstick: Rabblerouser Red.

It takes a shot of whiskey to get me out the door. I need that hot sharp burst for the courage to get me down the dark hall and through the ill-lit streets. I down another shot for an extra jolt of confidence and then I splash on some cologne and am headed for work.

I think about Veronica and what I will tell her. She, more than anyone else I know, will understand the pain that's cracking me apart.

Veronica hasn't seen her own little boy in three years, not since she left him behind in Manila to come to Japan and earn money for his support. The boy's father was a U.S. marine, a good old boy from Kentucky, and although he married Veronica, the marriage didn't last. He shipped out, leaving his ex-wife and child behind, and Veronica has heard nothing since.

Now, the boy lives with her mother. The grandmother sends the photos that Veronica shows me when we don't have any customers. The boy's milk tea eyes are shy. He is missing his front teeth. Sometimes they talk on the phone, and the next evening Veronica will show up with a heavily powdered nose and red veins shooting across her pupils.

I think about Veronica all the way to the club, and I'm able to put the pounding and the heavy footsteps out of my head. When I reach the entrance, my shoulders loosen. I let the breath flow out of my lungs.

Mama Morita welcomed me back, no questions asked, when I showed up on her doorstep a year ago.

"You're like a daughter to me," she'd said, embracing me. Hugs are rare in Japan, and I'd clung to her for a good five minutes.

I'd spilled my story—the full schedule of private English lessons that had dwindled into nothing, the unpaid rent, the threatened evictions. My empty refrigerator. All I had was a cupboard full of cans of Spaghetti-O's—Kei's favorite—that I was tending like a shrine.

"You can start working again tonight, if you like," Mama Morita had said. She patted my hand. Her heavy rings clunked against my knuckles.

And so here I am, a year later, still working as a bar hostess.

The other women are gathered, lounging on the cushioned stools, like a scene out of a harem. Veronica, in a peony-painted *cheongsam*, is in the back painting Betty's fingernails. How nice it would be if we could just lock the doors and drink and gab all night long without fingers creeping up our thighs. Without foul-breathed businessmen leaning into our faces.

The thought has barely entered my mind when our first customer of the evening breezes in.

We all go quiet at once. I hear a sharp intake of breath. I know it isn't Mama Morita. She is all charm as she floats to the doorway.

The man is wearing a gaudy aloha shirt, the short sleeves revealing intricately tattooed forearms. His hair is permed and a gold toothpick flashes at the corner of his mouth. I can't see his eyes behind the dark sunglasses. I feel like laughing because he is nearly a caricature of a Japanese gangster. But of course I don't laugh because I know almost immediately that he is here for me.

"Jill, why don't you keep this gentleman company." Mama Morita has her arm through his as she escorts him to my table. She nods to another hostess who busies herself preparing a tray of peanuts and liquor.

I know that I am relatively safe here. Mama Morita will be behind the bar, keeping on eye on things, and there are witnesses all around. I sit there and wait for him to speak.

He isn't interested in chitchat.

"I've heard that you've been bothering the Yamashiro's son."

He uses the word *"chonan,"* to indicate eldest son, heir.

"He's my child," I say. I should be scared, I know, but I feel as if I'm in a B movie, a comic book. The situation is beyond ridiculous.

Mama Morita sets a couple of drinks before us, and just to show this thug how little I respect him, I take a swig before he's even touched his glass. She's mixed them especially strong; the drink kicks in right away.

"Do you have any children?" I ask. "Do you have a son?"

He ignores me. "You're working illegally as a hostess on a tourist visa," he says. He looks around the bar, rests his gaze on the beautiful Veronica, on Betty with her vermilion fingernails. "And so are they."

The threat is clear. He means to have me deported, to destroy my benefactor's business. But I won't be cowed.

What I'm thinking is: My son is in the hands of crooks and I don't want him growing up in that house.

I decide to go along with him for now. I just want him to leave me alone. I bow my head, force tears into my eyes.

*"Wakarimashita,"* I say. "I understand."

He smiles then and I get a good look at all of his silver teeth. He downs his drink with one tip of the glass and then leaves without paying.

No one tries to stop him.

# 1989

MY SUPER HERO SURFERS STILL HANG ON MAMA MORITA'S WALL. There is another painting of mine in her house. It's of a little girl in costume for *Awa Odori*, the annual dance festival that takes over Tokushima in mid-August. I suppose it reminds Mama of her daughter.

I made the sketch from memory just a few hours before Yusuke came to my apartment for the first time. He was coming to see my paintings, he'd said, but I was planning to seduce him. Even so, I greeted him at the door in jeans and a cotton sweater. I'd painted my toe nails carmine—my only concession to glamour. I didn't want him to confuse me with the bar girl. After all, that wasn't the real me.

He bowed before stepping out of his shoes and up into my rooms. He'd brought a box of imported chocolates. I wasn't sure how to interpret his gift. Flowers or perfume would have been less ambiguous. Maybe he gave me chocolate only because he believed that foreigners didn't like the customary Japanese bean cakes.

He was wearing a subtly textured dark suit and a tie blazing with various shades of red. He was dressed, I thought, for a date, but then again, maybe this was what he wore for work. I caught a whiff of his neck, the musky cologne he'd splashed there.

"Welcome," I said. I led him to cushions strewn over the *tatami* floor.

I imagined us reclining upon them, as if in a seraglio, feeding each other the truffles. But Yusuke knelt, and I was forced to do the same.

I had my portfolio within arm's reach.

"I really don't have a lot of finished paintings with me," I said, "but I've made some preliminary sketches for some that I'd like to do. And I'm planning a trip to Arima next week-end for more."

Arima was one of the places that Blondelle Malone had visited on her trip to Japan. I was hoping to trace her route as much as possible. Before my fellowship expired, I would plant my easel in view of Mt. Fuji. I'd paint the harbor of Yokohama.

In Arima, a town known for its hot springs, Blondelle had been shocked to see men bathing naked. I thought of relaying this anecdote to Yusuke. Maybe he would laugh at her prudishness. Or, maybe he would think that I was being vulgar. I kept the story to myself.

I excused myself to make tea. I'd bought a little packet of plum tea with flecks of gold for this occasion. I hoped it wouldn't be too flashy.

Meanwhile, Yusuke leafed through my drawings. When he seemed to linger on one, I edged into the room, trying to figure out what had caught his attention.

By the time I'd returned with a tray, he'd closed the portfolio and was studying a picture I'd hung on the wall.

"Did you do that?" he asked.

"Yes." It was a salt marsh at sunrise. "When I feel homesick, I look there, and I can feel myself back in South Carolina."

"It must be a beautiful place," he said.

I started to tell him about the dolphins and the Spanish moss and the crepe myrtle. And then I caught something in his eyes that made me stop.

"This place can be very beautiful as well," he said quietly. "Wait till you see the cherry blossoms."

It seemed that he wanted me to like Japan, that maybe he wanted me to stay. I was moved to silence.

"I have already found many beautiful things here," I said. "There are many things that I'd like to paint."

And then there were the words that I felt I'd been waiting for my whole life: "I don't have anything planned at my gallery for November. How about if we give you a show?"

If this was just a line to get me into bed, he could have fooled me. He made no move to kiss me, didn't even brush my sleeve with his. In fact, we shook hands, and after a few more polite words, another cup of tea, he said his good-byes and left my apartment.

I had a lot of work to do, and I no longer had time to pour whiskey.

• • • • •

A couple of weeks later, Yusuke called and invited me to his gallery. It was a small intimate space, perfect for a cocktail party of elite connoisseurs or maybe a poetry reading.

On that day, he was showing furniture made of driftwood and fallen branches from the forest by an American artist. She'd gathered the wood along the banks of the Yoshino River and the beaches of southern Tokushima and fashioned chairs, hat stands, tables and sculptures.

"She's going to be famous," Yusuke said. "She's my discovery."

Like me, I hoped. In a few months I would hang my surfers and dancers and bunraku puppets and thatched roof houses on these walls. In the corner, I would display the painting I'd done just the week before of a pair of egrets wading in a rice paddy. And on the wall facing the entrance, I would place my rendering of the cliffs at dusk—the dramatic angles, bright light spearing the clouds.

I browsed around the gallery, taking peeks at the price markers on the wall near each piece. Everything in the room had been sold.

"People in the city hate to be away from the action, but they still want to connect with nature," Yusuke said. "They can sit in these chairs and think about being in the woods without having mosquitoes crawling all over them."

"They're beautiful pieces," I said, trailing a few fingers over gently sanded rungs. "They remind me of ikebana."

Each piece was asymmetrical, totally unique.

Yusuke nodded, as if he approved of my observation.

"How is your work coming along?" he asked.

"Good, I said. "I think I'll be ready." To tell the truth, I was nervous. I lay awake in bed at night, afraid of falling flat on my face. But I'd already discovered that everything I did was seen through a sheen of foreignness.

In Blondelle Malone's day, Americans and Europeans pounced upon anything remotely Oriental. Theaters staged dramas concerning geisha girls, novelists borrowed Eastern landscapes for their stories. Even the music world—look at Madame Butterfly— was obsessed with Japan.

Now, here in Japan, it was the age of Coca Cola, Madonna and the NBA. And although the glitz of Hollywood had reached the far corners of the archipelago, I'd discovered that the Japanese tended to worship minor characters. At the video rental store there was an entire shelf devoted to B-actress Phoebe Cates.

Japanese taste was something of a mystery to me. I thought there was a chance that the people here would actually like my work, if they only knew about it.

"I have a friend who writes for the local newspaper," Yusuke said, as if reading my mind. "I'll get him to interview you just before the show."

I nodded, feigning cool. I'd never been interviewed by a newspaper before.

After we'd spent a few more minutes in the gallery, Yusuke took me out to lunch. Then he said that he had to go help out at his father's construction company, and he dropped me off at the train station.

• • • • •

I hadn't seen or spoken to Eric since I'd stopped working at the Cha Cha Club, so I was a little surprised when he called a few days later.

"I'm having a party the day after tomorrow," he said. "Why don't you come?"

He said that it was in honor of Columbus Day, but I knew that Eric would use any excuse to tap a keg.

I thought about asking Yusuke to go with me, but I remembered that he was headed to Tokyo for the weekend. The trip had something to do with his father's company. Besides, if the Cha Cha Club crowd was there, he might not approve. I'd go solo.

The night of the party, at around six, I squirted my neck with perfume, hopped on my bicycle—a one-speed wonder with squeaky brakes—and wheeled off toward Eric's apartment. I bought a bottle of Beaujolais en route. He'd said that he'd be grilling steaks.

I could hear the reggae music from down the street. High-pitched laughter rang out. As I got a little closer, I could smell charcoal and beef.

The party had spilled from Eric's first floor apartment into the parking lot where the boom box and grill rested on asphalt. Some young Japanese, deeply tanned and in hippie clothes, were dancing to the music. I figured they were Eric's surfer friends. The others, pale-faced and mousy-haired like myself, were probably his cronies from the Happy English School. None of the hostesses were there.

I parked my bike alongside the building and grabbed the neck of the wine bottle. For a moment, I lingered at the edge of the gathering, feeling invisible, until Eric emerged from his apartment. He was wearing Ray Bans and his hair had been bleached by the sun.

"Jill!" He spread his arms wide for a hug.

I let him embrace me. We'd never been quite this friendly before, but he'd obviously had a few beers.

I handed over the wine.

A Japanese woman in sarong and bikini top stepped up behind Eric. She wrapped her arms around his waist and peeked at me over his shoulder.

"This is Aiko," he said. He pulled her around in front of him. "Hey, babe. Go get my friend here a drink." He patted her bottom as she went off.

I raised my eyebrows. "Whatever happened to Akemi?"

"Keeping track, huh?"

I shrugged. "It's a small town."

He adjusted his sunglasses and stretched toward the waning sun. "Akemi is a nice girl, but life's a banquet, man. C'mon. Dance."

I worked my way into the knot of surfers and spent a couple of songs grooving to Bob Marley. I had steak and corn on the cob and a beer or two.

Eric introduced me as an artist.

One of his surfer buddies asked for my phone number, but I told him that I had a boyfriend already. Not exactly true, but I was working on it.

I started thinking about Yusuke. He'd given me the number of his hotel. I dropped my crumpled beer can into the trash and went inside to call him. I found a phone in the kitchen. A few Americans were huddled around the refrigerator, bitching about their English-teaching jobs, but they took no notice of me.

A guy with wire-rimmed glasses started rolling a joint at the kitchen table.

"Holy shit!" Another guy in knee-length pants in a sort of aborigine print leaned over and inspected his work. "Where'd you get that? Man, you could be fucking deported. Remember what happened to Paul McCartney? He's, like banned from Japan. And he's famous."

"Relax. Do you think any of these yokels know what dope smells like?"

I turned away from them and dialed. Yusuke answered on the third ring.

"Where are you?" he asked. "It's pretty noisy."

"I'm at a friend's house. He's having a party."

"Eric?"

"Yes, as a matter of fact. How did you know?"

"I have my sources."

I laughed, flattered. He was interested in me after all. He'd been asking around.

"Eric has a new girlfriend every time I see him," I said. I didn't want Yusuke to think that we were somehow involved. "You'd better lock up your sisters."

"I don't have any sisters," he said. "I'm an only child."

He didn't ask why I was calling him in the middle of a business trip. He seemed perfectly comfortable just chatting with me. I wondered suddenly if he had been holding back because of Eric, because of what he had suspected between Eric and me.

"When you get back to Tokushima, I'm making you dinner," I said.

•  •  •  •  •

I started preparing for my date with Yusuke as soon as I got up the next morning. I hung my futon out over the balcony railing and washed the sheets, just in case.

Because all I had in my cupboard was an array of mismatched dishes, I went down to the little gift shop across from the post office and bought two Noritake china plates in a tasteful border design, and a pair of Bohemian crystal wine glasses. I even sprang for a couple of candlesticks and long white tapers. I bought a tablecloth and jacquard napkins.

Then I hit the bakery for crusty French bread, the fishmonger for fresh squid and scallops, and the supermarket for fresh vegetables. I followed a recipe I'd gotten from *Elle*—no "feed your family in 20 minutes" formula, but complicated secrets from a famous chef's kitchen. I nicked my finger with a knife while cleaning the squid. Otherwise, my preparations went well. I finished cooking with minutes to spare. By the time the doorbell rang, I'd showered and powdered and perfumed myself. I was wearing a black cotton knit dress.

Yusuke gave me a long look when I opened the door and

emitted a low growl. "You smell good." He handed over a bottle of wine and a pint of ice cream in a brown paper sack. Then he stepped into my apartment and took a deep breath. "Or maybe it's dinner."

We each drank a glass of wine on my balcony. I had a couple of chairs set up next to the washing machine. It was bold, I know—the neighbors could look up from the parking lot and see us there—but there was something romantic about the pink sky bleeding into ocean, the birds dipping and gliding on the evening breeze. We spoke softly, mindful of potential eavesdroppers, and then we went inside and had dinner.

I liked watching Yusuke eat. He closed his eyes after the first bite, as if he wanted to enjoy the flavor without any other distraction. I felt some kind of pride watching him sop up the garlic-tinged spaghetti sauce with his bread. I liked knowing that I could satisfy him. He filled his plate twice, and twice wiped it clean.

"Dessert?" I asked, when it seemed he'd had enough.

I took the ice cream out of the freezer and set it down on the counter and then started clearing away the dishes. Yusuke poured the rest of the wine into our glasses and brought a bowl to the sink. We were doing a little dance in the kitchen area, stepping around each other with smeared plates, the silverware jangling like tambourines. And then I whirled quickly and found myself in a tango embrace, my back arched over the linoleum.

He brought me slowly back up to a standing position, and then he scooped me into his arms. He carried me into the next room and lowered me onto the sweet-smelling reed mats. In the end, we didn't need the futon at all. The ice cream melted all over the counter.

# 1997

WHEN I CRAWL INTO MY APARTMENT AT 2AM, I SEE THE RED LIGHT OF my answering machine semaphoring in the dark. I'm not even tempted to listen to the message. It's probably the henchman calling for further harassment. I fall across my futon.

I sleep all day Sunday, my day off. On Monday morning, I heave myself out of my little nest and pick up the phone.

"Global Travel. How can I help you?"

The voice on the other end is way too perky, but I suppress my irritation.

"I need a reservation on a flight from Osaka to Bangkok," I say. "Anytime next month would be fine."

I don't have the cash to pay off my lawyer, but I do have enough socked away for a brief trip out of the country to renew my tourist visa. I can thank my shady visitor for reminding me that my current visa is ready to expire.

The quickest way would be to go to Korea, and the cheapest method would be by boat—ferries make the crossing on a daily basis—but I need a vacation. I need to go to a place that does not remind me of Japan. I have never been to Thailand before, but I imagine that it is dirtier, that the people are friendlier and the colors brighter.

After I book a flight, I pour myself a cup of coffee and get dressed. Eric will be here soon. His Monday morning visits are

50

a regular part of my weekly schedule. I'm basically his charity case.

To get to my apartment, Eric has to wade through a pack of stray dogs. There must be seven or eight. They're Akita hounds, the only kind of dog I've ever seen around here, with pointy ears and short honey-colored fur. I don't know what the big attraction of this place is, but they stick close to the building. They cavort among the bicycles, chase their tails in the parking lot, greet me every time I go down the stairs. Someone must be feeding them.

When I open the door, Eric is standing there with a sack of fresh vegetables from his garden. His white pants are printed with muddy paws.

"They were trying to get at the carrots, huh?" I say.

Eric steps into my entryway and unloads the sack in my arms. "Yeah, well, I tossed out an onion but there were no takers."

He slips out of his sandals, *zori* that he wove himself from rice straw, and sits down cross-legged on the floor.

"So how are you feeling today?" His voice is mellow and soothing like an NPR announcer. I know that he has noticed the empty beer cans lined up on my kitchen table, but he chooses not to mention them.

"Not too great," I say. "I called my lawyer last week and he said that I was stalking him."

Eric smiles. "And are you?"

"Give me a break." I run a hand through my hair, realizing that I forgot to comb it. "He said not to call him again until I've finished paying my bill. I personally think that there is more work to be done here. He's giving up too easily. I have not been served well."

"What do you want him to do, exactly?"

"I asked him to appeal."

"And what did he say?"

"That no one ever appeals decisions in divorces and that I will never get my son back."

"Sounds like you need another lawyer."

"You're right," I say. "Want a drink?"

I set a kettle to boil and drop a teabag in a cup. It's ginger, Eric's favorite. He doesn't say anything when I snap open a beer. It's early, but the hair of the dog really helps sometimes.

"You should come to my yoga class," he says, not for the first time. "I think it would help you relax."

"Maybe I will," I say, as I always do.

"I'm serious. You need to find a way to heal." He tosses his hand in front of him. As if he is flinging beans, I think. Beans for the festival of *Setsubun*.

"Out with the devils! In with happiness!" At the beginning of February, the advent of spring on the old Japanese calendar, children all over Japan chant these words and throw dried soybeans at someone dressed up as a demon. The beans supposedly drive the demons out and make way for happiness. One year, Yusuke donned a mask—a red-faced ogre with a yellow horn sprouting from its black-yarn hair—and Kei flung beans at him. If only it were that simple.

Eric seems to think that it is. Ever since he met that guru in Hawaii, he seems to believe that he has all the answers. If I stop eating cucumbers like he has, will I suddenly become whole again? If I decide to give up sex (not that there is any decision-making involved at the moment) will I find inner peace and derive daily ecstasy from the scent of flowers?

I can not always take him seriously, but he is kind.

"Here is your tea." I set the cup before him and take a swig of beer.

And so we pass the morning together, my oldest expatriate friend and I. Then Eric goes off to the beach because, he tells me, that waves are just right.

After he leaves, I notice that the red light on the answering machine is still blinking. For a split second, I consider erasing all of the messages without listening to them, but curiosity gets the better of me.

The first message is just a click, the sound of someone hanging up. The second is from Maya, my former next-door-neighbor. "Hi. Maya-chan *desu*. I finish report like you ask me to. See you at coffee shop tomorrow?" And the third. The third makes me suck in my breath and bite my lip. I have not heard this voice in a couple of years, but it is familiar, like a favorite song.

"Hey, Jill," the voice says. "This is Philip."

Philip. The one who broke my heart.

# 1987

I REMEMBER KISSING PHILIP IN THE RAIN. WE STOOD ON THE SIDE-walk under giant, dripping oaks, in full view of motorists cruising past. My sundress was wet, pasted to my body. I wanted to take it off right there, to roll with this man in the mud puddles, to pull him deeply into my body. I understood my feelings to be love.

We had already been together for six months. Philip's obsession with me had peaked. He was beginning to see my flaws, to look beyond them toward Africa. He had begun to be impatient when I called him, drunk, in the middle of the night, to recite a poem I'd found.

I was cultivating a persona then. I thought that as an artist I should be spontaneous and excessive. I thought that I could feel things more deeply than other people.

I had garnered confidence from Philip's early passion. He'd declared his love for me within a week of our meeting each other. I grew to love him for loving me. I wanted to marry him and give birth to five children that he, as the product of a large, crazy Irish-Catholic family, said that he wanted. At twenty-one, I was ready to sign my soul over to him. I thought that this was the deepest love that would ever come over me. I did not yet understand that it was nothing compared to what I'd feel years later for my son, for Kei.

Maybe, like the flare of my ardor for Philip, it has something to do with parting. For nine months, Kei lived in my body, matching his rhythms to mine. At birth, he left it. Everything afterwards was a move further away from me: the first time he reached out for his father, the first time he held a spoon and shoveled food into his mouth. His first step, though toward me, was a veering into independence.

• • • • •

Instead of attending my university graduation ceremony, I went to Boston to meet Philip's mother. Neither of us really cared about all the pomp and circumstance. The graduating class was large and it would take three hours just to hand out all the diplomas. And I figured that the keynote speaker, a has-been African American singer who'd been doing TV commercials for the past few years, would dish out the same old spiel about how we were the future of our country. Whatever.

No one in Philip's family would have been attending the proceedings anyway. His mother was busy with her law firm and couldn't get away. His brothers and sisters were scattered all over the globe—Elizabeth, in England, working at Barclays Bank and engaged to a world-famous sommelier; Kate, in Kenya, doing anthropological field work; her twin, Liam, in Russia, writing for an economic journal; Nuala, with successful lawyer husband and four kids in Connecticut; and little brother Gabe, working his way through med school in Charleston. They were all busy, all absorbed by their own lives. His father might have attended, might have taken him out for dinner afterward, but that's about it.

My family, on the other hand, was disappointed. My parents were big on rites of passage and they were upset about losing out on this chance to feel proud. My grandparents had been planning on making the sixteen-hour drive from Michigan to be there. Grandma, I found out later, had even sewn a new dress for the occasion. There would have been a sheet cake with my name in pink icing and mounds of presents and camera flashes going off every ten seconds. So I felt guilty when I got on that plane, felt guilty still when my feet touched the tarmac at Logan.

Philip was at the airport waiting for me, having driven up a few days earlier. He gave me a peck on the lips and asked about my flight.

"It felt like my stomach was going through the spin cycle," I told him, "but I think it was more from fear of meeting your mother than the hundred foot freefall over North Carolina."

He laughed then slung an arm over my shoulder and herded me toward baggage claim. "She'll love you. Trust me."

According to Philip, his mother had thought that his previous girlfriend had looked like "a bitch in heat." He'd brought her to Mummy's house in Myrtle Beach and then he'd never called her again.

The first thing I noticed about Mrs. McCarthy was her blonde hair. It was obviously dyed, and for some reason, this intimidated me. If she had been gently graying, like my own mother, I might have been reassured.

The second thing I noticed was her red-lacquered fingernails. They bit into my skin a little when she gripped my hand in greeting.

"I've heard so much about you, dear," she said. She smiled, but her eyes were cold.

The three of us had dinner together—take-out tabouleh and felafels from a Middle-Eastern deli down the street. I thought the menu was exotic, but I didn't say so. I was afraid of coming off as some kind of bumpkin. "It's delicious," I said.

"Isn't it, though?" she replied.

I felt as if she were waiting for me to say something clever, to prove to her that Philip wasn't lying, that I was just as fabulous as he'd said. She didn't seem like the kind of person who'd fall for gooey compliments.

I thought of saying something about the room with its tasteful, austere décor. There was no mess of magazines; the pillows were plumped just so; the lamps and furniture were devoid of dust, thanks to a once-a-week housekeeper.

"Mrs. McCarthy—" I began.

"Oh, call her Mummy," Philip cut in.

I thought I detected a faint grimace. Mrs. McCarthy was chilled by British reserve, unlike her son who had been steeped in American familiarity. Besides, the babyish appellation didn't fit this woman who smoked Cigarillos after dinner. "Mummy" would be a plump cookie baker, a woman with a generous bosom and a faded floral dress.

"Kate's coming over later," Philip's mother said.

"How is Kate?" Philip asked.

Mrs. McCarthy sighed. "I don't know. I wish she would get her act together. She might have stuck with it."

I remembered then that there had been some trouble. Kate had been mugged by an African with a machete and the resulting trauma had cut her internship short.

What kind of mother could Mrs. McCarthy be? I wondered. My parents would have demanded that I return on the first flight out of Nairobi. There would have been none of this sighing.

But Philip agreed with his mother. "Yeah, I'm a little worried about Kate."

I was primed for a basket case, a young woman with electric-shocked hair who jumped at the slightest sound. But Kate, who arrived thirty minutes later, looked entirely normal. She breezed in with a big smile for all. "Hi, Mummy! Philip! And this is Jill? How did you manage to snap up such a pretty girlfriend?" She was dressed in a long floral rayon dress that swept across her ankles, revealing fleeting glimpses of the butterflies tattooed there. She was hip, young, and beautiful with huge brown eyes and shiny bobbed hair. I liked her immediately.

In spite of her terrible experience, she appeared totally at ease. I was still a nervous wreck.

Philip went into the kitchen to help his mother make coffee. Kate sat on a stool near me, hugged her knees like a child and said, "So how did you two meet? I'm dying to know."

"We were in the same French class," I said.

Philip had been entirely oblivious to me at first. I sat at the back of the classroom, he at the front. Although we were in the same room three hours a week, he never acknowledged me when we happened to bump into each other outside class. I'd spent an hour almost right next to him at a rock concert on campus and although I'd waited for his attention to drift over to me, he'd never taken his eyes off the band on the stage.

One evening, I was sitting on a bench in front of the library, reading *Eugenie Grandet*, and he stopped in front of me and said "hello." I'd been even more surprised when he sat down and began talking to me. We talked for hours. I discovered that he was going to Senegal on a Rotary scholarship after graduation. I had a Peace Corps application in my apartment waiting to be filled out. I'd fallen in love with the words of Doris Lessing and Nadine Gordimer. I'd seen *Out of Africa* ten times. In the next hour, we found other similarities. We had both studied abroad in France and missed the epicurean lifestyle there. We both drove yellow Volkswagens (his a '72, mine a slightly later model), and we liked the same music.

I abandoned Balzac for the evening and joined him for dinner and a movie. By the time I arrived back at my apartment, six hours had elapsed. My blood felt full of bubbles; my head, of helium.

He told me two weeks later that he was in love with me. I was a little frightened by his intensity, but also exhilarated. I did not feel love. I felt, at first, ignobly, "This man is my ticket to Africa." He said as much: "You can come visit me in Dakar. I'll buy you a plane ticket."

Now, here was Kate with her painted ankle, back from Africa, smiling at me in Mrs. McCarthy's living room, shaking her head. "How can you put up with Philip? I think he'd make a terrible husband and I'm going to tell him that."

Here was the chance to dig out deep dark secrets and hidden tendencies. Instead, I said, "Well, he makes a wonderful boyfriend." And it was true.

Philip made tapes for me, brought me breakfast in bed, massaged my shoulders when I was feeling tense. He wanted marriage, kids, money, success, travel, and adventure. I wanted those things, too.

Later, after Kate had gone back to her apartment, the remaining three of us parted, off to separate bedrooms.

"No screwing around in my house, you two," Mrs. McCarthy had said when we'd first arrived. She'd said it with a smile, but I could tell that she meant it. I had been assigned to an extra bedroom, Philip to the foldout sofa.

I would have liked to sleep in Philip's childhood bed, to stare at the Red Sox pennants thumbtacked to the wall, clay monsters crafted by a boy's hands. But Philip's childhood must have been packed away in boxes somewhere, consigned to the attic or a storage shed after one of his mother's many moves. This was Mrs. McCarthy's house, and hers alone.

● ● ● ● ●

Eighteen hours later we were setting out on a double date. Mrs. McCarthy's escort was one of her colleagues, a hotshot lawyer from Chicago who was cousin to a famous actor. I'd had a crush on the actor ever since I'd seen him in his first big movie, a Vietnam action flick. I was hoping that the evening would be slightly silly so that I could ask questions about him.

As it turned out, the evening was not silly at all. Philip had chosen the restaurant—dark, hush-hush, with a view of the river. The menu was in French and he persuaded his mother to let him order for everyone. I was glad. I knew that his pronunciation was better than mine. I liked to listen to the R's scrape against his throat. I didn't want my tongue to get tangled up before an audience.

The wine arrived and Philip did the tasting. "*Superbe*," he said.

I tried not to lunge and gulp from the crystal. I was wearing silk and make-up, but it felt like a disguise. My heart was suddenly twelve years old.

The lawyer, Ben, was nice, slightly teddy bear-ish. He had a paunch and jowls.

"So, Philip, Jill. Any big plans now that you're out in the world?"

Philip jumped right in. "First, there's Senegal, of course. Then I'm thinking law school. Harvard, maybe. Or Yale."

Mrs. McCarthy nodded.

"Jill?"

"I'm going to be an artist."

"Do you mean a graphic designer?" asked Mrs. McCarthy, her brow knit in confusion.

"Well, no. I'm hoping to follow in the footsteps of Blondelle Malone, who at the height of her career was dubbed 'America's Garden Artist' by the *New York Times*—"

"Blondelle who?"

"Blondelle Malone." I could feel my face getting redder and redder. "She was a landscape artist. She went around the world painting the gardens of aristocrats."

The diamond studs in Mrs. McCarthy's lobes caught the candlelight as she shook her head. "My dear, I don't see how you are going to make a living painting pictures."

A weird silence fell over the table. My eyes flickered to Philip, but he said nothing. He was studying his potage, suddenly a botanist intent on floating parsley.

Just as I felt the first prick of tears behind my eyes, Ben lifted his wine glass and said, "I propose a toast to the graduates."

Three more glasses rose into the air.

"To Philip, the future legal eagle, and to Jill, America's next garden artist."

The kiss of crystal rang out. I lapsed into silence for the rest of the meal.

• • • • •

The following afternoon we were outside, sprawled over a checkered cloth. I had brought my graduation present, a Minolta 35mm camera and I peered through the viewfinder, framing possible photos: Here was Philip, schmoozing at the family picnic.

Uberparents Nuala and Ted and their brood of four had arrived from Bridgeport. Their children were tumbling in the grass, having already devoured their sandwiches. They had brought along friends—a French couple and their curly-haired toddler. Philip was speaking with Monsieur, a stockbroker on Wall Street. Bits of their conversation drifted over.

"Any chance of a summer internship?" Philip asked. He was not leaving for Dakar until September, nearly four months later. He would be busy making connections and money until then. Earlier, Philip had admired Monsieur's BMW in the driveway. "*C'est une belle voiture.*"

I knew that it didn't matter to Philip if he was a lawyer or stockbroker. What he really wanted was success. Money. A shiny German car like the one out front. A beach house on Sullivan's Island or Nantucket. And that was what I told myself I wanted, too. If I could hold Philip's attention for just a little while longer, I would be able to fly to Senegal, live in a grand house, have beautiful things. As much as I loved his long, lanky body, his endless energy and enthusiasm, I also loved the lifestyle he represented.

• • • • •

That night I was lying awake in bed when the door opened silently. There was Philip, a murky mass sneaking toward the bed. "My mother likes you," he announced in a whisper. "She thinks you're a lady."

I tried to smile. Somehow, I couldn't take that as a compliment. Mrs. McCarthy would probably have liked me better if I jumped out of planes or skied down steep mountains. If I was attacked in a dark alley by a man with a knife and I slugged my assailant, maybe then she would consider me worthy. I was becoming giddy with these thoughts. I giggled. Philip hugged me, probably thinking that I was relieved to have passed muster.

• • • • •

After I left Boston, after I met Philip's mother and two sisters, I waited for him to call. He didn't. He sent a postcard from Myrtle Beach—the Grand Strand, a stretch of sand with elbow-to-elbow sunbathers—and a terse note saying that he was working ten hours a day at a seafood restaurant. He was busy. He hoped that I was okay.

I wondered if his mother had said something about me, or if he had met someone else. A waitress. A tourist. I remembered his story about the ex-girlfriend, the one his mother had said looked like "a bitch in heat." I wondered if this is what had happened to her. There was no easy explanation. On my last night in Boston, we had made love, and it was as intense as it had ever been. And then Philip had said, "I want to be with you again as soon as possible."

I had a dream one night that Philip was a mass murderer. I watched as he sliced up a baby. In the dream, I was horrified. There was basic human fear, and also the horror of knowing that I was in love with him and I could not save him. At the trial, he walked by laughing like a lunatic and pronounced himself "not guilty." I was sick, knowing that he would be convicted and executed. I woke up feeling a terrible love for him. Meanwhile, he was doing a hatchet job on my heart.

In July, two months after I'd last seen him, I finally called him. It was before noon, before his shift at the restaurant. He sounded tired.

"So," I said. "Am I going to see you before you go to Senegal?"

"Yeah, of course."

"How about the day after tomorrow?"

"The day after tomorrow? Hmm. I don't know."

"My dad and step-mom are going to the Bahamas for a week. We could stay at their house, hang out by the pool. What do you say?"

I thought I heard a sigh, but I wasn't sure. When he replied, it was with conviction, if not enthusiasm. "Okay. I'll drive up after my shift. It'll be late. I probably won't get there till two, three o'clock in the morning. Is that alright?"

"I'll leave the porch light on for you."

He was going to give me twenty-four hours and that was better than nothing. I went shopping the next day and bought steaks for grilling. I marinated shiitake mushrooms and baked a marble cheesecake. Philip was big on food. He had once insisted that I listen while he read me a rave review of a restaurant in the *New York Times*. There was little or no possibility that we would ever be eating there, but he exulted in every word, seemed to taste the descriptions.

So I made all of my grand preparations and then I began to wait. I sat by the pool for awhile, watching the moon's reflection ripple on the water. Then, when the mosquitoes began attacking me, I moved to the living room. I poured myself a glass of wine and opened a novel. He had not yet arrived by four, so I went to bed, leaving the front door unlocked. I smiled to myself thinking that when I woke up he would be beside me. But he wasn't.

I opened my eyes at seven. The phone rang a few minutes later.

"Jill, hey, sorry. I had a little accident round about Conway."

"An accident?"

"Guess I fell asleep at the wheel. Car rolled over three times. Man, if I hadn't been wearing my seat belt, I'd be dead."

"Whoa. Are you hurt? Are you in the hospital?"

"Naw, I just got back. My head hurts, but looks like nothing's broken. No internal injuries."

"Well, that's good. How's the car?"

"Totalled."

It occurred to me that we would no longer be driving the same make of car.

"Hey, why don't you drive down here? We can find some way to salvage the week-end."

He asked, so I went.

I drove three and a half hours with the windows down, hot wind blowing through the car. I jammed a cassette he'd made for me a couple of months before in the tape deck and listened to

63

the lyrics, trying to decipher hidden messages. My little car flew through the small towns along the way—Horrell Hill, Hannah, Salem, Nixonville, Wampee—and then I found the turn-off for North Myrtle Beach. I followed the directions he'd given me till I arrived at a two-story beach house with peeling blue paint.

I could smell the ocean as soon as I got out of the car. The sound of the waves slurping at the shore carried over the low dunes. The house looked abandoned. No one had peeked out the window to see who'd arrived. I had to knock.

Philip was sharing the place with a couple of other waiters. One of them, a blond guy with dreadlocks, opened the door.

"You must be Jill," he said. He yelled over his shoulder for Philip and motioned me inside.

When he came into the room, I watched his face carefully. He smiled in what I thought was a sad way, then opened his arms to me.

I moved into his embrace. "Does it hurt?" I asked, tightening my hold on him.

"A little. Hey, have a seat. Do you want something to drink? Beer? Iced tea?"

All I really wanted to do was fall into bed and sleep. I told him this and he drew me by the hand to his room. It was dim and spare—a mattress on the floor, a stack of Economics textbooks in the corner, his waiter uniform hanging from the doorknob. I let him unzip my sundress and ease it over my hips. He yanked off his T-shirt, revealing a pear-shaped bruise on his left side. And then we both climbed under the crisp white sheets and made slow sad love.

In the afternoon, we went to the beach with a cooler of Dos Equis and a quilt and lay in the sun for a few hours, barely speaking to each other. Once in a while, we rinsed off in the cool water, and emerged licking salt from our lips. I wanted to feel happy— happy that Philip was alive, at least, happy that we were finally together again, but I couldn't. Ice was forming in my bowels. My stomach wouldn't settle.

When Philip had had enough sun, he suggested dinner at a favorite restaurant. I liked the place for its breezy informality. We sat on a deck outside. There were buckets under the table for shucked shells and a roll of paper towels next to the salt and pepper shakers for sopping up clam juice. We ate steamed oysters sprinkled with hot pepper sauce, drank one more beer, and topped it all off with Key Lime pie.

I had taken one bite of pie when I couldn't stand it any longer. "You've stopped loving me," I said. "Haven't you?"

He didn't answer at first. He looked off toward the salt marshes, watched an egret lift on its great white wings into the sky. Then he nodded ever so slightly, ever so slowly.

"Goddamn it." I knew that I was about to cry and start a scene, but I couldn't help it. My fatigue and all that beer and hot sun had rendered everything surreal anyway. "You weren't going to ever call me, were you? You were just hoping I'd fade away. Why the hell did I go to Boston anyway?"

"Hey," he said. "I don't know about you, but I had a damn good time this past year."

I wanted to smash the rest of my pie into his face, but of course I didn't. Instead, I pushed the plate to the center of the table and stood up. I walked off, fully intending to leave him there.

He caught up with me at the car. I stood with my forehead pressed to hot metal, willing myself not to cry.

"Don't go like this. At least spend the night. Get some rest."

I wanted closure. I wanted him to explain at what point and for what reason his feelings had changed, but he had already ruined my memories of a year. Every sweet and beautiful thing he had ever done would be forever tainted by this outcome.

I stayed the night because I wasn't sure that I could make it all the way back without rolling my car just as Philip had done. Suicide wasn't on my mind. The beginnings of rage were sustaining me just then. I slept next to Philip, in his bed, careful to keep a few inches between us.

As soon as the sun came up, I slithered out of bed, grabbed my stuff, and headed back for Columbia. I didn't write a note or kiss his forehead. He slept, oblivious to my leaving.

For the rest of the summer, I tried to paint what I felt. One big canvas was covered with thick gouache question marks in various shades of gray. In another, I painted myself the way I looked after crying, my face all splotchy and swollen. When that didn't help, I visited a shrink. She wrote out a prescription for Prozac and sent me on my way.

I ran into Philip a couple months later at Goatfeathers, a place that we'd gone to as a couple. He was sitting in a booth near the door where we'd once shared a piece of Mississippi Mud Pie. Some young woman that I'd never seen before was seated across from him. She was skinny and she had a big nose.

"Hey," Philip said. "How's it going?"

"Alright, I guess." Could he tell that I'd lost ten pounds? Grief had made me slender.

"This is Genevieve," he said, nodding to his companion. "She's over from Aix."

Aix-en-Provence was where Philip had studied. I wondered if this woman had been his lover. He'd once mentioned sleeping with someone on a ski trip to the Swiss Alps, but we had never spent much time discussing past relationships. Maybe he had lied and I wasn't his first great love after all. Maybe this Genevieve had been between us all along.

"Nice to meet you," I said flatly. Just greeting them was exhausting. I started to move away from their table.

"I'll call you," he said.

"You do that."

He phoned from the airport, just before he left for Africa, and then he wrote me a letter from Dakar. He wrote about studying Wolof and his new friend who made drums and about riding in a Jeep across the desert. There was no mention of us.

I responded with anecdotes about the people I worked with at the public library, where I'd been hired as staff artist. I wrote about the homeless woman who checked out books on witch-craft and the famous writer who dropped in one day to make a speech.

He wrote in later letters about the beauty of Sierra Leone, about being detained by soldiers in Liberia and having a gun shoved in his face while he fended off allegations of CIA involvement. Exciting stuff to be sure, but not what I wanted to read.

I stopped writing to him. End of story. I decided to go to Japan.

# 1997

MY EX-HUSBAND HAS HIS PROFESSIONAL BULLY, AND I HAVE MY SPY. Her name is Maya Kitagawa. She's sixteen years old and lives two doors down from the house where I lived with Yusuke, the house where my son lives now with his father and grandmother.

I knew she would be perfect for the job when I ran into her at a shopping arcade. There she was with her friends, all of them sporting the same brassy hair and glittery eye shadow. They were dressed alike in obscenely short pleated skirts and slouchy knee-high socks. Only Maya had a Chanel watch strapped to her wrist, though. And she was the only one of the three with a Louis Vuitton bag swinging from the crook of her elbow.

I'd sipped tea with Maya's mother a few times during my career as wife, and I knew the Kitagawas were not the type of parents to outfit their daughter in expensive labels. And since Maya herself had often complained to me about her measly allowance, I figured that she'd either gotten a high-paying job (not likely), or she'd secured a sugar daddy.

At any rate, when I asked her to keep an eye on Yusuke's house, she was more than willing to help out. I think she sees herself as the heroine in a cloak-and-dagger drama.

Although she could easily report to me via cell phone, she prefers our cafe meetings. On this day, when she walks in I am already sitting in my usual seat, in a corner, away from the window.

She looks over her shoulder and then hurries to our table.

"Did anyone follow you?" I ask in a low voice. I try to make it as fun for her as possible.

"No," she says, still breathless from running across the street. "I don't think so.

"Good. Now what have you got for me?"

She unlatches her book bag and pulls out a notebook. She always writes her reports down in English. I think it's risky to put any of this in writing at all, but she claims that this is her cover. She'll say she's having me check her English composition for class, if anyone—my former mother-in-law, for instance—stumbles upon us. Besides, she always says, no one else in her family can read English anyhow.

In spite of her shady after-school activities and her looks—the spiky bangs falling over her eyes, the iridescent lip gloss, today's knee-high vinyl boots—she is a serious student. We first met when she came knocking at the door, looking for an English tutor. Her reports are always written neatly.

I watch her open the notebook and smooth down the pages with her hand. She sits up straight, clears her throat and begins reading.

"The day before yesterday, grandmother go out at five p.m. without Kei. I think she go shopping."

I have to stop myself from correcting Maya's grammar. "She left him alone?"

"Yes. She go out and I see Kei in the living room watching TV."

Well, this is good news, I think. I would never leave my six-year-old son alone in the house—what if there was a fire?—but her irresponsibility could work in my favor. I let out a stream of air.

"Anything else?"

"I think Mr. Yusuke maybe have a girlfriend."

Her words punch me in the chest. "A girlfriend?" So soon? In the year since our divorce I haven't even been on a date. Is he trying to find a replacement mom for Kei? "Why do you think that?"

"I smell perfume in his car. Guerlain, I think."

"In his car? You were snooping around in his car?"

I'm thinking now that Maya is going a bit too far with her sleuthing. She's going to get us both in a lot of trouble.

"Um, yes. I mean, no. Not snoopy. He give me a ride during the rainy day."

"And you smelled perfume."

Maya nods. She looks up at me from under her bangs, and I can tell that she is nervous. She thinks that I am angry with her.

I attempt a smile. "Good job. Is there anything else? Does Kei go to cram school? Does he have music lessons or something?"

"I think maybe *soroban*. My mother said so."

I reach into my purse for the envelope I have prepared. "Okay, try to find out what day he goes to abacus class and where. And maybe try to find out more about this girlfriend." Then I slide the envelope containing five thousand yen across the table.

Maya picks it up with two hands, holds it in the air, and bows her head for a moment. "Thank you very much," she says.

"You're welcome."

• • • • •

About once a month, Veronica and I have dinner together. We take turns cooking comfort food for one another. For me, it's often macaroni and cheese, mashed potatoes, eggs scrambled with smoked salmon.

On this evening, we sit in Veronica's impeccable apartment—no dust to write your name in here—the windows pushed open to welcome sea air, Filipino pop music spilling from the stereo. We stretch out on *tatami*, our heads cushioned by *zabuton*.

Veronica's got a dish of adobo on the stove. The vinegary aroma reminds her of Manila, the place that she calls home.

"Do you think you'll ever go back?" I ask her. We've had this conversation before. It's almost a ritual by now.

"Someday," she says, twining black hair around her hands. Her red fingernails peek out from among the strands. "How about you? Do you want to go back to your country?"

"Someday." I almost tell her then what I've got planned. I'm bursting to confide, but it's a dangerous thing. I stopper my mouth with a beer bottle and take a long swig.

And then we move on to our next favorite topic, our dreams of true love.

"He'll be tall," Veronica says. "A basketball player."

I stretch out, admiring my glitter-painted toenails. "Mine will look like Mel Gibson in *The Year of Living Dangerously*." I giggle. "He'll write haiku all over my body. With his tongue."

Veronica wrinkles her nose. "That's just sex. I want somebody who'll make chicken soup when I'm sick in bed. A guy who will help Luis with his homework and teach him how to fix a car."

I nod. It's been awhile since I've been laid, so I tend to get distracted. "I want a guy who will pick his socks up off the floor and send me roses once a month. He'll take me up in a hot air balloon, show me the universe."

Veronica goes over to the refrigerator and gets herself another bottle of beer. She pries off the cap and takes her drink to the window, looks out to sea. Our momentum is lost.

"His birthday is tomorrow," she says, barely a whisper. "He'll be nine. Can you believe it?"

I reach out and touch her shoulder, feel her wilting under my fingers. "Men," I say softly. "Who needs them anyway?"

But the thing is, we do need them. We need them sitting on those worn, crushed velvet chairs, sucking up drinks, sharing their million and one woes so that we can take their money and pay our rent, save up for plane tickets and long-distance phone calls.

The next evening, Veronica and I are both a little hung-over from too many beers, depleted by confessions. But we put on our make-up and our almost-silk polyester dresses and arrange ourselves at the bar.

The first group to come in is from the Board of Education. They're already wobbly and as red as ripe strawberries from an earlier party. Mama Morita guides them into a corner and they flop into chairs, loosen their ties, and being passing around the songbook.

Veronica goes over with a little notebook to write down their selections. One guy with a bad toupee tries to pull her onto his lap, but she swats his hand away. "*Dame, dame,*" she says, waggling her finger. "Be a good boy now."

Betty and Yoko start pouring whiskey. The more these guys drink, the more money we make. We've devised a repertoire of drinking games, some recalled from my American university days. Betty takes a coin out of her pocket and I see that she's about to engage them in a round of "quarters."

I'm still sitting at the bar, nursing a seltzer. Mama Morita is saving me. She's got four Filipinas, but I'm the only American.

A couple more groups come in—bankers and then some insurance guys, and then there's only one hostess left. Me.

The door swings open again and a man steps in. He's rather portly with thinning hair. His eyes, behind dark-rimmed glasses, turn down at the corners giving him an air of perpetual melancholy. Unlike our other customers this evening, this one walks in sober. He stands in the doorway looking slightly bewildered, but only for a heartbeat. Mama Morita glides over as soon as she sees him and takes his arm. She settles him at a table. He sits facing outward with a view of the room. Before he has time to feel lonely, I sashay over with a smile.

"*Konbanwa.*"

He half-rises and bows. "*Dozo, dozo.*"

I wonder if this is his first time in a hostess bar.

"How about a whiskey?" I ask.

He nods vigorously and I get to pouring drinks. "Karaoke?" I ask, proferring the songbook.

"No, no." The guy actually blushes. "*Uta ga heta.*" I can't sing.

"Well, then," I slide into my Marlene Dietrich bargirl croon. "How about if I sing something for you?"

He nods again, even more vigorously than before. "That would be fine."

We engage in a little more chitchat till my number comes up.

Veronica brings the mike over, leaning just enough for my guy to catch a whiff of her perfume. He gazes up into her face, into her smile, and blinks a few times. He watches as she whirls away from us, back to the table with the superintendent of schools. He stares at her while I sing "Yesterday." That number is always a safe bet. At least once a week, we get a Beatles fanatic in here, some guy who knows all the lyrics on the *Abbey Road* album, or every detail of Paul's drug bust. But Shima-san doesn't appear to be one of them. His eyes are still on Veronica when I sit back down beside him.

"Shima-san," I say, pressing a hand on his arm. "How about if I refill your glass?"

He turns to me as if waking from a dream.

• • • • •

Shima-san comes again three nights later. This time, he's early, the first customer of the evening. Mama Morita goes over to greet him, confers and nods. She shows him to a table and resumes her place behind the bar. "Veronica," she says, nodding toward the guy. "This one's for you."

They sit at the table under my painting of the surfers. Shima-san gives it a glance and I am inexplicably happy that he notices it. I want to tell him myself that at one time I wasn't just a bar hostess. I was an artist with the world at my feet. I was invincible in love. When exactly did it all start to go so wrong?

73

# 1989

ON THE EVENING OF THE OPENING, MY VERY FIRST ART SHOW, I forgot that I was in a small town in the provinces of Japan. I felt as if I might have been in New York or Tokyo, as if the reporters who interviewed me were from glossy art magazines, not the *Tokushima Shinbun* and the *Japan Times*.

I dressed in black—a simple sheath—with a boa tossed over my shoulders.

Yusuke nodded his approval when I walked in the door. He kissed my neck, just below the earlobe. "Later I'm going to take that dress off of you," he said.

"I hope so."

We were alone for just a few minutes. The guests started coming at a little after seven, and by seven thirty, everyone had arrived. Parties in that town had a definite beginning and end. No one could start drinking until everyone had gathered and Yusuke had delivered his speech.

He raised his glass and began going on about Mary Cassatt and Paris, making me into some kind of expatriate icon. It all went to my head, along with the wine and my desire for him. I floated through the evening, laughing at jokes that weren't funny. I poured on the charm.

It must have worked. By the time everyone had gone home, Yusuke said that my paintings were sold. Every single one. I couldn't wait to get back to my easel and start painting again.

# 1990

AT THE END OF THE RAINY SEASON, MY NEIGHBORHOOD WAS filled with the beat of drums. Usually at night after dinner, I'd hear the endless repetitive melody, almost tribal. I knew that men and women and children were practicing for the summer festival, Awa Odori, which would be held in mid-August. It was likened to Mardi Gras in Rio di Janiero, but with more clothes.

"It's an excuse for people to get really drunk and fall down in the street," Eric explained.

"Do you dance?" I asked.

"Sure. Every year I've been here."

Already the town was plastered with posters of women in traditional costume—the pink summer *yukata* and the hats of woven straw. They wore lacquered clogs during the dance. I'd tried on a pair once and found them excruciatingly uncomfortable. So that's why they need to drink while dancing, I'd thought.

Yusuke had been talking up the festival as well. He was going to take me, he said. He'd even teach me the dance.

I was looking forward to the end of rain, to the fireworks, to the teams of dancers, but I was often on the verge of tears. My grant was running out. My year-in-Japan was almost finished. I'd have to go back to South Carolina soon. After that, I figured Yusuke would paste me into his mental scrapbook. He'd marry a Japanese woman.

The first night of the festival, we walked along the river,

browsing in stalls garlanded with lights. Men in short *happi* coats sweated over grilled corn-on-the-cob and fried octopus balls. Young men tossed rings, aiming for stuffed animals for the girl-friends who hovered expectantly. And little kids in festival garb carried plastic bags of goldfish, or slept slung over their fathers' shoulders. The night was noisy with drums and the calls of touts, the drunken laughter of the dancers and spectators.

Conversation was impossible, so I just walked beside Yusuke, enjoying the brush of his hips against mine, the occasional meet-ing of our hands. He checked my face from time to time to make sure I was having fun, and I gave him the brightest smiles I could muster. Part of me wanted to drag him off into a shadow where we could be intimate, holding hands with no self-consciousness. I wondered how many people actually thought that we were a couple.

We stopped off at one booth and had a couple of beers. It was hot. I could feel the sweat dribbling down my back. My hair was beginning to smell like roasted corn. I plucked at my sundress, pulling it away from my damp skin.

And then, there, in the middle of all those people, Yusuke said, "Don't leave."

"What?" I thought that maybe I'd misheard him, or at least misinterpreted what he'd said.

"Don't go back to America," he shouted. This time he leaned closer. "Stay here. With me."

I forced a laugh. "I don't have a job. My visa expires next month."

He kissed me in the middle of that throng. I had never seen a Japanese couple kissing in public, and the act felt obscene. But when he stepped away no one seemed to be watching.

• • • • •

We eloped. At the end of summer, we got on a plane, flew to Hawaii, and married next to a waterfall in a private garden scent-ed by plumeria. Our witnesses were the ukelele player and the wedding planner, who'd managed to pencil us in on three days' notice.

There were other couples around, Japanese couples, here for a quickie no-sweat wedding/honeymoon. Some were with entourages—family and friends crowding in the edges of photos; others, like us, alone. Some people came here to save money.

For me, it was an act of urgency. I couldn't bear to be separated by an ocean from Yusuke. His name was inscribed on my soul and although we hadn't known each other very long, it was long enough. After all, I knew a Japanese couple who'd married three months after their first arranged meeting. They weren't even in love with each other.

My mother would be annoyed later when she found out that she wouldn't have a hand in choosing colors for the bridesmaid dresses, but she'd get over it. She and my father might even be secretly relieved to not have to foot the bill.

For Yusuke, I'm sure that it was an act of rebellion, a way of circumventing his parents' almost certain rejection of me. A last ditch attempt at independence from the octopus arms of his family, the duty. But I didn't let myself think of this at the time.

Instead, I signed the marriage certificate with a shaky hand. My heart was galloping, the blood singing in my veins. I felt as if I was acting in a movie.

After we'd said our vows, promising "till death do us part," we stood on the lawn sipping champagne and nibbling slices of macadamia nut cake. And then the sun was blurred by clouds and it started to rain. We dashed into the waiting Rolls Royce, part of the wedding package, and were whisked from the hills of Oahu to the airport where we boarded a small prop plane bound for Kauai. There, the honeymoon commenced at a lavish resort. We dangled our feet in the pool that evening, totally oblivious to what was waiting for us back in Japan.

• • • • •

I didn't expect his mother and father to be happy. I wouldn't have been surprised if they'd turned me away at the door. But although they must have been in a state of shock, they welcomed us home. After all, Yusuke was their only child. And we had nowhere else to go.

"It'll just be temporary," Yusuke said. "Until we build our own place."

Yusuke's mother set out slippers for me in the entryway. "When Yusuke called, we were very surprised," she said in a calm voice. "But congratulations."

She prepared a great feast for us—slabs of steak as well as the traditional congratulatory *omedetai*, red snapper curved in rigor mortis as if it were in mid-leap; bowls of steaming soup, with morsels of the rare Matsutake mushroom floating on top; red beans and rice; pickled radishes. Next to my place she laid out silverware, as if she doubted my ability to use chopsticks.

Her husband poured sake into thimble-like cups and made a toast in ornate, formal Japanese that I couldn't understand. He seemed, if not entirely happy, at least resigned. When he had finished speaking, he nodded to me and said in English, "Welcome to our family."

I bowed my head in gratitude.

Yusuke's mother watched as I tossed back a mouthful of the hot rice wine. Then she inclined toward me and laid a soft hand on my arm. "Do you have some news for us?" Her gaze flickered over my mid-section.

• • • • •

I wanted to be a good daughter-in-law. I wanted Yusuke's parents to like me. As we lay on our side-by-side futons that night, I turned to my new husband. "What should I call them?" I asked.

"Who?"

"Your mother and father."

"Okaasan and Otousan."

I remembered how Philip had suggested that I call his mother Mummy and the grimace she'd made. I wondered if Yusuke's mother would bristle in the same way. Probably not. She was Japanese, after all, and trained not to betray her emotions. Plus, she seemed nice. She'd prepared all that food. She'd laid out our futons and placed a sprig of lilac in a vase in our room.

"Well, what should I do tomorrow morning? Should I get up early and help your mother make breakfast?"

"Yes, that would probably impress her," he said. His voice was barely a mumble as he drifted toward sleep.

I wanted to shake him awake. I needed a crash course in how to behave as a Japanese wife under the eyes of his parents. Was there a book on the subject? A class at some college?

I'd heard that knowing how to arrange flowers improved a girl's chances of a good marriage. And if I'd studied tea or how to dance with a folded fan, Yusuke's parents might consider me refined. Maybe they would like my art. I decided I would paint a picture for them.

The next morning I managed to rise at six and my new mother-in-law, who was already awake, showed me how to make miso soup. The trick is to stir in the thick bean paste just before the water boils. (She had a special strainer and a spoon just for miso.) Then you add something that floats, like mushrooms, and something a bit heavier, like carrots.

"The colors are important," she said, as I watched silently.

I was used to jam slapped on toast, a cup of coffee on the side. After making miso soup for the first time I felt kind of tired.

And then we made an omelet. I thought I knew how to make an omelet: scramble some eggs, dump them into a heated fry pan, sprinkle with cheese and fold over. The Japanese version was more complicated. The eggs, sweetened with sugar, had to be cooked in a special pan and then rolled and sliced. If I ever had to make breakfast alone, I figured I'd have to get up at least an hour earlier.

But the eggs and soup weren't the last of it.

"Shall I show you how to prepare Yusuke's lunch?" she asked.

His lunch? I'd always assumed that he'd dropped in at some coffee shop for a sandwich or a plate of curry and rice. I'd never dreamed that his mother had been making his lunch all this time.

Without waiting for my reply, she pulled a two-tiered lacquer box out of the cupboard. Yellow chrysanthemums stood out against the shiny black lid. It was beautiful—the kind of thing that I would keep jewelry in. Or love letters.

"The rice goes here," she said, scooping some from the cooker into the lower tier. (She'd prepared the rice while I was still sleeping.) With a pair of chopsticks, she plucked a pickled plum from a container and set it at the center of the rice. It looked like the Japanese flag.

"And here, you should arrange bites of other things. Think about color. Think about beauty."

She brought some foods out of the refrigerator—meatballs in teriyaki sauce, nuggets of fried chicken, a flowerlet of broccoli, carrots cut into stars, wedges of apple. She motioned for me to put them into the box.

I pretended that this was art. While she watched, I deposited an island of green here, a hint of orange there. I tucked a piece of fish into the box. A few flowers were on hand, and I placed those carefully, too. When I'd finished, I stepped back and let her have a closer look.

She took up the chopsticks and jabbed around a bit, moving a cherry tomato, and then nodded.

I put the lid on the box.

But I wasn't finished.

Lastly, she produced a square of textured rayon, a *furoshiki*, and showed me how to wrap the carrying cloth around the box. Finally, corners securely knotted, we were ready to call the men to breakfast.

• • • • •

No sooner had Yusuke and his father left for work at the construction company, than his mother and I were out the door with a basket of laundry. I started to toss a wet towel over the bamboo pole, but she touched my arm and shook her head. She picked up another towel, and glancing over to make sure I was paying attention, snapped the wrinkles out, folded it precisely, and draped it over a hanger.

She instructed that my bra, Yusuke's briefs, and other "unmentionables" were to hang where the neighbors wouldn't be able to see them. I'd never given so much thought to laundry before in my life.

Next, we dragged the futons out of the bedrooms and into the sun. I noticed that we were the last in the vicinity to do this. A neighbor woman was sweeping her front porch. When she'd finished, she sloshed a bucket of water over the cement steps and then began washing the door. On one level, I admired her thoroughness, and that of my new mother-in-law, Okaasan. On another, I wondered if I would ever have a chance to paint as long as Yusuke and I were staying with his parents. I knew that I would never be able to keep up these standards once we were living on our own.

I decided to look upon that first day as a rite of passage. I had to prove myself to this woman who'd most likely dreamed of a very different bride for her son. So, when she motioned for me to get down on my hands and knees to wipe the floor with a thick towel, I thought, "Haven't you heard of mopping?" but I didn't say it. I polished the wooden floor until I could nearly see my reflection in it.

In the afternoon we took a break. Yusuke's mother went to her Ladies English class at the community center and I was left to my own devices. I took a nap and didn't wake up till it was time for dinner.

We sat down at the table—Yusuke, his father and I. His mother was still at the stove, flitting from countertop to table. I waited for her to join us, but she didn't. Yusuke's father slapped his hands together, said "*Itadakimasu*"—I shall partake—and took up his chopsticks. Yusuke did the same.

"What are you waiting for?" Yusuke's father asked me. "Eat up while it's still hot."

I knew that I should have been at the stove with my mother-in-law, settling for leftovers, the dregs of the soup, but I couldn't bring myself to join her. In my own family, no one had taken a bite until we were all gathered at the table. My mother had never jumped up mid-meal to prepare another dish.

Yusuke's father drained his cup of sake and held it out to me for another serving. I reached for the pottery bottle and refilled his cup with warm liquor. The cup was tiny, holding only a gulp or two. I expected to be busy throughout the meal.

Meanwhile, the fish on my plate stared up at me. It was getting cold.

My American manners were out of place here. Maybe they were considering me rude for not digging in with gusto as I had the night before. I sighed, sprinkled soy sauce onto the fish, gave it a squeeze of *sudachi,* and took a bite.

There was no conversation that night, only the sound of cracking jaws and clicking chopsticks. The sizzle of oil in a skillet, the gurgle of boiling water. I wanted to talk about something, but then again, maybe Yusuke's parents preferred silence during an ordinary meal.

By the time Yusuke's mother finally sat down, his father was probing his mouth with a toothpick. As she lifted her first bite of rice, he lit a cigarette. We were soon dining beneath a cloud of smoke.

After dinner, I helped clean up, took a bath, made love with my husband, and fell asleep. The days went along like this.

● ● ● ● ●

My mother-in-law pursued hobbies—ikebana, English conversation and quilting. When she was off at one of her classes, I luxuriated in solitude. The silence. Or sometimes, as soon as I heard the click of the door, I rushed to my easel and began painting wildly, splattering color on the sliding paper doors.

On the days when there were no lessons, I would try to go off on my own, but she often called me back for a tea-and-rice-cracker break in front of the TV. She was addicted to the gossip shows delving into the minutiae of celebrities' lives. Although I didn't know anything about Japanese entertainers, I tried to show interest.

"Who's he?" I asked, one afternoon, as we watched a man weep on screen.

"He's a very famous comedian," she said gravely.

I could tell from the crying, the black clothes, and the huge crowd that this was the funeral of someone important.

"His mother died," Okaasan said. "He was a good son. He took care of her."

•  •  •  •  •

I had a hobby of my own—visiting model homes. There was a small village of them, constructed by different companies (although none by the Yamashiro family enterprise which concentrated on larger projects) within cycling distance of the house. In the afternoons, when the floors had been shined and the last of the laundry folded and put away into drawers and closets, I sometimes grabbed my sketchpad and camera and pedaled off to see a new house. I only entered one per visit so as not to confuse them in my mind and because I enjoyed the tours and didn't want to run out of houses any time soon.

They were all grand, all beyond the average salaried employee's means. I didn't know of anyone who could have afforded the three-story mansion with elevator or the Scandinavian-inspired model featuring a cedar-walled sauna. But it didn't matter, because they weren't for sale. These were fantasy houses and no one would ever inhabit them. Eventually, they would be torn down and replaced with newer models, freshly imagined.

Gradually my own dream house was taking form. I sketched details that I liked—a bit of lattice, an indoor rock garden—and worked them into the plan. In the evenings, I showed Yusuke my drawings. Sometimes he was too tired to do much more than grunt, though other times he'd say he liked something or concede that it was a possibility.

"When do you think we'll be able to start building?" I asked one night.

I'd seen a house that day with an American-style deck and I imagined us having barbecues there.

Yusuke sighed as if I'd been asking him that question twenty times a day. In reality, I'd said nothing until then. I'd waited and watched, hoping for a clue as to how much longer I'd have to play at being the perfect Japanese housewife. I was beginning to lose patience. I was sick of washing doors.

"I'll talk to my parents about it," he said. "Just give me a little time."

But then suddenly everything changed.

• • • • •

I'd just returned from visiting another model house. I'd been particularly taken with the curving bay windows in the sunken living room and the twist of the cast iron stairs. In my mind, I was already telling Yusuke about the Italian Plexiglas sink in the bathroom. I grabbed the door handle and yanked. Although we never locked the door during the day, it didn't give.

I rang the doorbell a few times, to no avail, and then went around to the back door. I found the spare key hanging on a nail beneath some onions, and let myself into the kitchen. The light was on and a teakettle whistled furiously.

"Okaasan?"

No one replied.

I turned off the heat and the light, then went from room to room looking for her. She was gone.

Although I was mystified, I have to admit that relief whooshed through me. Without her there to judge and supervise, I could sprawl across the *tatami* mats, bury myself in a novel, or take a nap. I could paint.

I had no idea when she'd be back, but I rushed to set up my easel. I'd been thinking of painting the view from the second floor—Mt. Bizan sloped like an eyebrow in the distance, the sparkling river, the blue tile rooftops shimmering in the late afternoon rays.

In the first few minutes I was jumpy and alert, sure that I'd be interrupted. There was probably some dusty nook she'd want me to sweep out. But gradually, my concentration deepened. Everything became color and light.

When the phone rang at around five o'clock, it took me awhile to notice. Even when I did, I chose to ignore it for awhile. After all, who would be calling me? But the phone kept ringing and ringing.

It was Yusuke. He was crying.

"My father is dead. He had a heart attack at the site. You'd better vacuum the big *tatami* room."

His words made no sense at first. I finally figured out that he and his mother were bringing the body home and that relatives and colleagues and neighbors would soon be gathering for a wake.

Later, I watched an ambulance pull up into the driveway. Yusuke got out of the car, followed by his mother, who leaned heavily on the arm he offered to her. She seemed to have shrunk since that morning. She was suddenly very old.

I rushed out to meet them, but they brushed me aside. Yusuke's mother was sobbing loudly. Finally, Yusuke motioned that I was to help carry his father's body into the house.

Two men from the hospital hoisted the shrouded corpse out of the back of the vehicle. I slipped my hands underneath. I could still feel the heat of life, even through the sheets and clothes. His weight was like an anchor, threatening to drag me down.

# 1997

IT IS MIDNIGHT AND I AM THREE-QUARTERS THROUGH A BOTTLE OF Beaujolais Nouveau. I'm marinating in memories. The photo album is splayed open on my knees, everything blurry through a scrim of tears.

Here is Kei at two, in *happi* coat and *hachimaki*, tired from the festival. I remember the hot breath of the night, the fireworks blooming in the sky, sparkling and shattering, boom boom and then chandeliers raining down, pink chrysanthemums, shooting stars, or comets rising toward the moon. All along the road, cars like ours were stopped bumper to bumper, edging into the lane. Passengers stood outside their vehicles, silent, watching. The moon was full, fat, white as pure butter. The smell of coals, a barbecue, animal piss. The bridge full of cars, a chain of lights that dazzled like jewelry. Mount Bizan hovered across the river. Kei pointed and said, "Mountain."

And in this picture, Kei sits at my mother's Formica counter with a bowl of canned spaghetti. I could have made it myself, but I'd loved it as a child, and I wanted to share all of that with my son: Spaghetti-O's and Kool-Aid and Twinkies and Charlie Brown and Scooby Doo and Halloween. I wanted him to ride the coin-operated horse in front of Kroger's and color in cheap-papered books with Crayola crayons.

I'm so deep in the past that when the phone rings, I grab it off the hook without reflection. "*Moshi, moshi.*"

"Hey, big girl. You're a hard one to get a hold of. I've been trying for days."

Those Boston vowels, still strong after Paris and Hollywood and Mexico City. That sense of urgency. I can almost see his knee bobbing. He was always in motion, jittery and fidgeting, unable to thoroughly contain his energy.

"Hello, Philip. How are you?" I reach for my wine glass, but topple it instead. The *tatami* will be stained. "How did you find me?" I ask.

"Your mother. How else?"

"So where are you? The connection is so good, his voice so sharp, that he could be across the street.

"Indonesia."

A quick trip across the sea. An hour by plane from Bangkok.

"I'm bringing movies to the masses."

He's in marketing for 20th Century Fox. He's living in a high rise in Jakarta. I ask him if he has a maid, a chauffeur. He does.

"What about Jennifer? Is she with you?"

"Oh, man. She left me. She couldn't decide if she liked boys or girls."

"Well, there's a twist." I can't help but feel vindicated.

He tells me that his lover has taken up with a Mexican film-maker, a woman who looks a bit like Frida Kahlo with butch cut hair.

"So you know who Frida Kahlo is?" I tease.

"Hey. I know a little about art."

I don't tell him that I'm no longer painting. I don't tell him that I've lost my son. I'm thinking that this is one of those drunk-en, middle-of-the-night phone calls that some men make to ex-girlfriends when they are lonely. But I don't mind. I'm pretty damn lonely myself.

"Well," I say. "Now that we're both in Asia, maybe we can have lunch together sometime."

I can feel his grin through the line. "How about next week?"

"I'll see if I can pencil you in."

I tell him that I'm going to Bangkok soon to renew my visa. We make some vague plans, flirt a little, and then I find myself on my hands and knees, sopping up spilled wine.

# 1990

WITH THE MOON, CAME THE RELATIVES. YUSUKE'S AUNTS AND UNCLES and cousins from Osaka and Kyoto. Others, from the interior mountains of Shikoku. Some were from Tokushima City, but I'd never been introduced to them. I was meeting these people for the first time and try as I might, I couldn't get the names to stick to the proper faces. At first, I was confused about the connections.

But as they all gathered in the *tatami* room where Otousan was laid out on dry ice, I started to get an idea of who they were. After they'd had their moment of kneeling at my father-in-law's side, weeping or not, filling the room with reminiscences or paying their respects in silence, I served them tea. I tried to make eye contact with the aunts from Osaka, but they would not look at me.

I'd heard them talking to Okaasan in the corridor and their tone was not friendly. They seemed to be blaming her for Otousan's death. He was their brother, and she was the country bumpkin they had never found quite good enough for him. The niece-in-law—me—an embarrasing mistake, a blemish in the family line.

Okaasan's siblings were in cheap dark prints and spoke heavy *Awa-ben*, the dialect that city people laughed at when they heard it. I realized, watching them, that Okaasan had made herself over.

She wasn't born speaking behind her hand. Even her gait was acquired, I thought, watching her sister lumber up the driveway.

Okaasan didn't speak to her sister much, nor to her two brothers who kneeled with their wives at the rear of the room. Obviously they weren't close, but they had still managed to turn out for their brother-in-law's wake.

Yusuke stuck close to his mother, speaking to me only to tell me to change into something black. When I told him that I was sorry about his father, he gave me a blank stare.

First there was tea, and then beer and whiskey. Yusuke poured for the uncles and male cousins. He drank along with them, his face and neck turning a deep red.

Once, when he got up to get a new bottle of beer, he leaned close to me and whispered, "You're doing great. I'm proud of you."

My legs were numb from so much kneeling. Cigarette and incense smoke burned my eyes. Fatigue caused cramps in my joints. But I kept myself awake in that room, even as various relatives curled up in corners, heads cushioned by *zabuton*, and began to snore.

At midnight, Yusuke, his mother and his father's siblings dressed the body in a white kimono. Then they lifted and rotated the body so that it was facing north, the direction of the land of the dead.

The night crawled and then it was morning.

After breakfast, the aunts helped to wash the dishes, then all the women laid out their black kimono and began disrobing. The men were in another room, shaking off hangovers and changing into mourning wear. I had no proper clothes of my own, so I was renting a black suit. I sat in my black tunic and leggings at the kitchen table waiting for it to be delivered.

I was sitting there still, drinking sour coffee, when Yusuke walked into the room. The skin around his eyes was puffy and the wrinkles in his forehead more pronounced than usual, but that wasn't what made my glance snag on his face. His cheeks were suddenly smooth, except for a tiny piece of toilet paper sticking to his jaw. He'd shaved off his beard.

Now he looked like any other salaryman on the streets of Tokushima. His face was ordinary. He seemed like a stranger.

• • • • •

With the death of his father, Yusuke became the head of the Yamashiro household. I figured that made me something. My position had been elevated. Okaasan was now the dowager, a behind-the-scenes figure like Hirohito's widow or England's Queen Mother who sat back while her daughter and grandchildren sucked up all the publicity.

I no longer felt inclined toward obedience. I began devoting my mornings to art, and six months later I had enough paintings to fill the gallery again. This time I made up the guest list. I invited Mama Morita, who'd been the first to buy one of my paintings, and her employees. I also sent a post card to Eric who, as far as I knew, was still surfing and teaching English at the Happy English Conversation School. I wasn't sure if Yusuke's friends had bought my work as a one-time favor to him or not, but I invited them anyway. I assumed that Okaasan would have no interest in a stand-up cocktail party.

Yusuke helped me to hang the pictures, commenting as he did on their wistful tone. I'd used a lot of grays and deep blues. I'd painted last-burst-of-glory sunsets, rice at the end of the season, a girl waving to a boat as it sailed away. I thought my technique was improving, and if no one bought the paintings I'd hang them all over the Yamashiro house.

One of Yusuke's art buddies was trying to explain the concept of "*wabi-sabi*" to me in broken English when Eric came through the door. His blond head bobbed over the sea of black, toward me. I excused myself and turned to meet him.

"So where's your date?"

He chucked me on the shoulder. "Didn't bring one. Women!"

I raised my eyebrows.

"You don't want to know," he said. "I got involved in a nasty love triangle. Nearly got my balls cut off." He covered his groin for emphasis, then laughed. "I'm going to Hawaii in a couple of days on an extended surfing safari. Gotta get away from this madness. Hey, where's the beer?"

I led Eric to the bar at the back of the room and put a drink in his hand. One of the hostesses appeared at my elbow.

Without her usual make-up and the clingy dresses she wore for work, there was a quiet elegance about her. She'd come in billowy pants and tunic, her skin and shape concealed. When she moved, she seemed to float.

"Jill." She embraced me and then gestured to the painting of the girl waving to a boat. "I understand her feeling. I want to buy this picture."

I wondered if she saw herself standing on shore as the boat left her behind, sailing back to the Philippines. And why would she want to be reminded of her homesickness? But I didn't dwell on this for too long. I'd sold a painting. She was already digging for her wallet. I directed her to Yusuke's secretary, who was taking care of the finances. "You'll have some pocket money," Yusuke had said.

Yusuke, my Stieglitz, chatting up my brilliance on the other side of the room, sliding me an occasional glance, a wink, debonair in his Comme des Garcons suit. For day, he wore conservative navy blue, cut like a businessman's uniform. He went about with his smooth cheeks and short hair, instilling confidence in all the old men who decided when and what to build—those men at city hall, the presidents of companies bursting through their present walls, ready for bigger, more modern digs, a reflection of boom-time success. He played the part well, I was sure. He carried responsibility on his shoulders, held it there still when he walked in the door at night, the Heir of the House of Yamashiro.

But here, away from the teak desk and the men with cash in their pockets, the cranes and bulldozers and dumptrucks, the holes in the ground at the birth of a new building, here, he was another person. He was the Yusuke of the beard and a love of blue. His movements were soft and fluid, his laugh genuine. This was where he belonged—with me, in a room full of color and people who cared about shadows and lights. He belonged in that suit with a drink in his hand, with vintage David Bowie coming through the sound system and a million stars shining down.

An hour later, Eric was teetering. I smelled something acrid and forbidden.

"You didn't bring any illegal substances here, did you?" I looked closely at his eyes, but they didn't seem especially red.

"Your husband seems like a nice guy," he said, ignoring me.

I murmured in agreement.

"He runs a construction company, right?"

I nodded.

"So does he have yakuza connections?"

"What are you talking about"

"Well, everybody knows that construction companies use gangsters to round up cheap labor. The yakuza treat the day laborers like indentured servants, but they keep them in line. The cops need the heavies to control the workers, so they look the other way."

I just stared at him for a moment.

Eric went on. "Or maybe your husband's company has been putting up buildings for yakuza. They're into real estate these days."

"What, you mean money-laundering?"

He shrugged. "They don't call it that here. It's just business."

"I'm sure Yusuke doesn't have anything to do with organized crime," I said. "Maybe you've had a little too much to drink."

"Sorry. Just making conversation."

"Get this man a cup of coffee," I said to the man standing next to me, "and then call him a taxi."

I didn't sell everything that night, but I made enough money to buy a plane ticket, for example. In case I wanted to get out of there. But I didn't. I wanted to stay.

After the guests had gone and Yusuke had locked up the gallery, we walked down the deserted street hand-in-hand, trying to make the moment last.

# 1991

ONE MORNING I STOOD AT THE KITCHEN SINK, STARING OUT THE window. Buds were forming on the plum trees. A swallow flitted in the eaves, then swooped away. Tears came to my eyes and I didn't know why.

Chop chop chop. The sound of Okaasan's knife sliced into my reverie. Thunk of steel against wood. In an instant, she'd rendered a stalk of green onions to tiny circles, a block of tofu into thimble-sized cubes.

I looked down at my hands, my idle hands, and then moved to put the salmon slices on the grill. Then there was the click click and whoosh of the gas stove coming to life, followed by the odor of fish flesh. I retched.

"*Daijobu?*" Okaasan pushed me into a chair.

My head was suddenly swimming. I bent over and wedged it between my knees, the blood crashing like a storm.

"*O-mizu kudasai,*" I managed.

She murmured something and brought me a glass of cold tap water. I held it against my damp forehead for a moment before taking a few sips.

"I'll do this," she said, with a glance at the stove. "Go back to sleep."

I dragged myself back up the stairs to where Yusuke still lay, nestled under the futon. I slipped in beside him and closed my eyes.

"What happened?" he asked, his voice rough with sleep.

"I think I'm going to throw up," I said. And then I did.

Yusuke wet a cloth and pressed it to my forehead. "There's something going around," he said. "Some guys on my crew are sick, too."

I nodded against the pillow, but I already knew that this was not just the flu. I believed it was a symptom of my psychic state, the manifestation of a sickening soul. I'd been a trooper all this time, I thought, and now all of my repressed anxieties were coming to get me.

I was wrong.

A week later, Okaasan drove me to see a doctor.

"Congratulations," he said, as we sat in his office. "You're pregnant."

• • • • •

I was at a natural food store, looking for some ginger tea to quell my nausea, when I felt someone standing behind me. At first, I didn't turn to look. It was probably some English junkie wanting to practice a few words on me, I thought. I picked up a box of imported chamomile tea and read the label.

"Having trouble sleeping?" The voice was familiar.

He was standing behind me with a big grin.

"Eric! Your hair!" He was not quite bald, but close. His scalp shone bristles. He looked leaner, too. I wondered if he had been sick. "Did you join the army or something?"

"Not quite. An Ashram."

My jaw dropped. "You?"

He laughed. "Don't look so surprised. I'm doing yoga now, too. I'm actually teaching it down in Yuki."

We went to the back of the store and sat down at a little table. Over cups of lemon mint tea and carob cake, he told me the story of his amazing transformation. It seems he'd gone to Hawaii in search of big waves and found big wisdom instead. On a lark, he and a friend had climbed a volcano to meet a kahuna who'd immediately diagnosed all of Eric's spiritual ills.

"He told me that I should stop eating cucumbers," Eric said, "And that I should redirect my sexual energy."

"You've given up sex?"

"Yup. And now tell me about you."

I laughed. "Quite the opposite. I'm pregnant."

His face lit up. "Really?" He pulled me out of the chair and gently waltzed me down the soymilk aisle. "That's wonderful. Congratulations."

I blushed. I hadn't dreamed it would make Eric so happy.

"Can I touch?" he asked, reaching toward my stomach.

I was just starting to show. I hadn't yet felt those first kicks or prods. "Yes."

Eric crouched down in front of me and laid both hands on the small bulge that was my baby. I could feel the heat of his skin through two layers of clothing. I wondered for an instant if it was fever and everything he had just told me was caused by delirium. But I had to admit there was a new vibrancy about him. When his fingers brushed mine, a spark jumped between us.

"I'll bet it's a boy," he said.

"Are you psychic as well?"

He chuckled. "No, it's something my grandmother always said. If the mother carries low, it'll be a boy."

He had spent weeks in Hawaii, absorbing the teachings of his mountain mystic before going on to India. He would still be there, he said, if not for a dream he'd had of Yuki. A vision, really, full of beautiful crying women.

I figured they were the owners of the hearts he'd broken on his earlier sexual rampage. He interpreted it differently. "There is suffering in Yuki," he said. "And I realized that it was my duty to come back and do something about it."

I nodded, trying to keep a straight face. Without a doubt, his yoga class was filled with attractive women, young and old, who wanted to have sex with him. In spite of his prickly head, he remained model-gorgeous. And although we were just friends, always had been, always would be, I entertained myself with a flicker of a fantasy of crawling across the table and ripping his clothes off. Blame it on hormones.

• • • • •

A week or so later, I woke from a nap and went downstairs to get a glass of water.

Yusuke's mother was in the kitchen, preparing a tray. She'd filled a lacquer bowl with individually wrapped rice crackers and arranged two short glasses next to a bottle of Kirin beer.

"Who's that for?" I asked.

"Yusuke has a guest," she said in a low voice.

"I'll take it in," I said.

She hesitated. For a moment, I was afraid she'd tell me that I wasn't allowed to make public appearances with my slightly swelling stomach, or that the weight of the tray would be too much for me, endangering her as-yet-to-be-born grandchild. But she must have decided that, yes, it was my role, after all. Hers was to be the matriarch, mine the galley slave.

I lifted the tray and headed for the receiving room. I heard a deep rumbling voice before I saw his face. The man was wearing tinted glasses. He had thick gold rings on two or three fingers of each hand and, because he was unusually expressive, I noticed them at once. He waved his hands around, catching and diverting light with his rings. One digit of his left pinky had been hacked off. He seemed to be telling a story. When he finished, he choked out a phlegmy laugh and fell back against the sofa, his hands suddenly still, pressing down on his knees.

Yusuke laughed along with him, but he was more restrained. Fake laughter, I thought. He's just trying to be polite.

I shifted then and the glasses tinkled together on the tray.

Both men turned and saw me.

A curtain fell over Yusuke's eyes, but he quickly recovered. "My wife, Jill," he said.

"She's beautiful," the man said. No "Nice to meet you" or "How do you do?"

I wasn't supposed to be there. I set the tray down between them and hastily excused myself.

My mother-in-law gave me a strange look when I bumped into her in the hallway. I told her that I was going back to my room.

Later that evening, when we were getting ready for bed, I asked Yusuke who had visited.

"A colleague," he said

"He works at a construction company?"

"Something like that." He avoided my eyes.

"A rival company?"

Yusuke sighed and then turned to face me. "Look, it was business. It's nothing that you need to worry about."

I wanted to cry out. I wanted to argue that everything that happened in that creaky old house concerned me because I was his wife. His family. And the heir or heiress to the company was swimming in my womb even then.

Instead, I lay in wounded silence, wondering how much I really knew this man.

• • • • •

Night, again. I'm listening to the chirping of tiny frogs in the rice paddies, the muffled blare of my neighbor's TV. A siren in the distance.

I think of the one time I rode in an ambulance, Mother-in-law beside me, crunching my hand in hers. She had never touched me like that before. I wanted to wrench my hand away, but I was frozen with terror.

All that blood on the bathroom floor. Was I about to lose my baby? If I moved, even a fraction, even just my hand to extract it from her grip, would I forever dislodge my son, The Heir?

The siren screamed us up and down the streets of Tokushima, through stoplights, around curves, and through the gates of the university hospital. No matter that I had picked out a midwife already, a kind lady who was known to serve strawberries to brand new mothers. I'd imagined her sopping the sweat from my forehead with a gauze pad. Instead, we were in an old building with stained ceilings and cracked walls, but with new machines and semi-famous doctors. Famous in that prefecture, at least.

"This is where I had my gall bladder removed," my mother-in-law said. "You'll be fine."

She followed alongside the gurney as best she could. She took little mincing steps as if the length of her stride were restricted by a kimono. Perhaps that was the effect she'd intended. I could almost see the silk banded around her legs. Running would be inelegant. At any rate, she managed to keep up with the emergency technicians and then the nurses as they raced me down the corridor and onto the elevator. I was afraid she'd follow me into the examination room, but one of the nurses showed her to a chair.

I hoped she'd go home, but I knew she wouldn't. If anything bad happened, if I lost the baby, I didn't want to share my grief with her. I needed Yusuke. I'd called him at work and left a message with the office girl. For all I knew he was at some faraway construction site, the ring of his cell-phone lost beneath the rumble of backhoes.

Just then a doctor came in. A young doctor. He looked to be in his thirties. The mid-wife was at least fifty. I figured she had decades of experience. But this guy.

"Hello!" He bounced over to me and thrust his hand out for a shake. (A little too much coffee this morning?) "I'm Dr. Ohara, Chief of Obstetrics and Gynecology."

My own palm was sweaty from fear, but I offered it to him. I noticed that he didn't wipe his hand on his scrubs—a point in his favor. He snapped on some rubber gloves and got down to business.

A few nurses hovered around. I pegged a couple bystanders as medical students. They all watched as the doctor globbed gel on my mound of a belly and turned to the monitor to check the ultrasound.

"See the heart beating?" Dr. Ohara clapped me on the shoulder.

"He's still in there, but you're going to have to stay in bed for the rest of your pregnancy."

I nodded. I'd do anything. I'd stand on my head for two months if I had to.

The doctor completed his exam, and then I was hoisted back onto the gurney by the students and nurses and wheeled into the corridor.

Yusuke's mother was immediately at my side.

"Where's Yusuke?" I asked.

"Is the baby okay?"

"Is my husband here? Is he coming?"

"What about the baby?"

I patted my stomach lightly. "He's still alive," I said. "Now what about Yusuke?"

• • • • •

I was assigned to a ward with three other women, thin blue curtains the only concession to privacy. As I lay there trying not to move, I could hear three different television shows, three different sets of visiting relatives and friends, and the deep sighs of my mother-in-law.

By the time Yusuke arrived, at least two of my roommates were snoring softly. Visiting hours were over. One TV emitted periodic laughter.

I heard the curtain draw open and saw him. His shoulders sagged. His mouth was tight. "Hi." He dropped a kiss on my forehead. "I'm sorry I didn't get here sooner."

"Why didn't you?" I wanted to say. Or, "What could have been so damned important that it couldn't wait until tomorrow?" But the weight of the day crashed down upon me then and I began to cry. "I was so scared," was all I could manage.

Yusuke sat down on the edge of the bed and tried to curl his body around mine. "He'll be fine. He's a Yamashiro, after all." He grinned. "And you're pretty tough, too."

When I'd wiped my tears away, I showed him the printed images from the ultrasound, the white swirls in the dark of my womb. And then I gave him the list I'd made of things that I would need.

First, I wanted him to bring my sketchpad and pastels and drawing pencils. I thought of Frida Kahlo painting in her bed after a back operation. I'd seen a photo of her once, propped against pillows, cigarette in one hand, brush in the other. She'd spent a lot of time in bed—recuperating from polio, then after the terrible accident in which her uterus was speared and ruined, and then after all those operations on her back.

She was a cripple, an invalid, yet she'd managed to lead a life of passion. There was her famous marriage to Diego Rivera, the muralist, and her affairs with Leon Trotsky and Isamu Noguchi.

Noguchi had lived on this island for awhile. He liked the stones he found on Shikoku. He had a studio north of here that Yusuke had promised to take me to see. But of course that wouldn't happen for some time. I was confined to bed and while I wouldn't be indulging in any physical passion, I intended to be as productive as Frida Kahlo.

When I wasn't painting or sketching, I'd study kanji. I wrote down the names of the books I'd need for learning the Chinese characters. I'd already mastered about five hundred. I figured I'd have learned another sixty by the time my son was born.

I needed a few novels and perhaps a book of poetry.

The list also included toiletries and special foods. I asked him to bring a couple of silk scarves, too, that I could tie around my hair or neck. I probably wouldn't be having a bath for awhile and I wanted a little something to help me feel like a goddess instead of a great, beached manatee.

He folded the paper and put it in his shirt pocket. Then he picked up the hairbrush on my nightstand and began to brush my hair.

In the morning he brought everything I asked for and I began to forgive him, a little. And so I was reading *Enigma* for the fourth or fifth time, when Yusuke's mother showed up that afternoon with a pile of bath towels and a canvas bag of tangerines.

"Oh, no, no, no," she said. "No reading!"

I put down the book for a moment, my thumb marking my place.

"It's bad for the baby," she said. "Reading excites the mind."

My book was hardly a thriller, and I knew what happened on every page since I'd read it before. I could have told her that I was reading more for inspiration and confirmation than excitement, but I wasn't sure she'd understand.

She reached out and I handed it over, thinking that she just wanted to peruse the back blurbs. I was wrong. She unloaded the fruit and shoved the book into her tote bag.

"No reading."

I didn't remind her that I was confined to bed for two months and that there wasn't a great deal to do while I lay there. "What should I do, then?" I asked, trying to be patient and reasonable.

"You should be calm and think about your baby."

I nodded slowly. As if I didn't think about him all the time. As if I could remain calm with her bursting into my hospital room whenever she felt like it and confiscating my books.

I closed my eyes and pretended to sleep. I could hear the clacking of her knitting needles, but I didn't open my eyes to see what she was making. I imagined that she was fashioning a scarf for Yusuke, or a pair of socks to leave at the altar of her dead husband. A little sweater or cap might jinx my pregnancy.

After a few minutes, I really did fall asleep. When I woke up later, the nurse was bringing my supper on a tray. Mother-in-law and my biography of Blondelle Malone were gone, but there was a pyramid of tangerines next to the TV.

• • • • •

The first time Kei was taken away from me was on the night he was born.

I was in a room with three other pregnant women—one, the veteran of three miscarriages, two others expecting twins. After a few nights together, we'd gotten to be friends, of a sort, though

I doubted I'd be seeing any of them once we left the hospital. Sure, we'd exchanged addresses, promising to send each other New Year's cards with pictures of our babies. Sure, we'd told each other embarrassing stories about gynecological exams and husbands. We'd created a slumber party atmosphere that wouldn't survive in the real world.

That night, the night that Kei was born, Mariko, who was expecting a boy and a girl, suddenly squealed, "Let's order a pizza! I'm hungry."

Well, we were pregnant. If we weren't puking, we were craving. Without a word, the rest of us reached into our pocketbooks and started scrounging up odd bills and change. Since we weren't allowed to walk to the cash dispenser in the lobby, we sometimes ran out of money. But we had enough that night for a large German potato salad and curry sauce pizza, and another topped with pineapple and corn.

Mariko placed the order on her cell phone and we started licking our lips in anticipation.

"Too bad we can't get beer to go with it," Risa, the other twin woman said.

"Yeah, beer would be good," Tamaki chimed in.

Just thinking of a frosty mug of Asahi Super Dry made me want to pee. The day before, the nurse had given me clearance to use the toilet just outside our room. I scooted out of the bed and, using my I.V. pole for balance, wobbled to the door.

I hadn't walked in a couple of weeks. Even those few steps exhausted me. I yanked down my pants, practically fell onto the toilet, and let out a scream.

My bleached white pregnant lady underpants were splotched with blood. More blood was gushing into the toilet bowl. Perspiration oozed from my pores. I fumbled for the nurse call button and leaned on it till someone came.

The nurse looped one of my arms over her shoulder and guided me back into bed. I felt like a wounded soldier, stumbling from the battlefield. I could see my roommates through a kind of haze, could feel their horror, but I didn't have it in me to explain what was happening.

The nurse went to page the doctor, and then returned with a wheelchair. The pizza delivery guy was right behind her. I could smell the spices in the sauce.

"Save a piece for me," I managed to joke. I wondered if Mariko, Risa, and Tamaki had any appetite left at all.

Soon I was lying on a table, under the ministrations of an intern until the real doctor arrived and pushed him aside.

"We're going to have to perform a C-section," he said in careful English. To the nurse, he added, "Call her husband."

I had prepared for natural childbirth. Although Yusuke was usually too busy to practice breathing with me, too busy to attend Lamaze classes at the community health center, I had readied myself. In my bag, there was a tape of Celtic harp music that I'd felt would be soothing. My plan was to have champagne on ice before I went into the delivery room. And while I wasn't so sure I wanted Yusuke video-taping the blessed event, I did expect him to be there.

But he wasn't.

Twenty minutes later, I was in a roomful of strangers, their faces hidden by blue gauze masks. One of them told me to curl up into a ball. A needle slid into my spine. I felt the wash of antiseptic over my middle, and then a few minutes later, the slice of the scalpel, but it didn't hurt. And then a wriggling, like a fish flopping, and the doctor said, "It's a boy. Very handsome."

I caught just a glimpse of his wet black head before he was whisked away. He disappeared behind doors. The nurse began to stitch me back together.

• • • • •

"Why won't they let me see him?" she asked. "Why can't I see my grandchild?"

I explained for the tenth time that only parents were allowed in the NICU.

"But I'm his grandmother!"

She only had to wait a week to see him. Other babies, hooked up to respirators and multiple I.V. drips, were hospitalized for months. But after seven days, I told her that Kei would be coming home.

"Tomorrow?" she wore a look of distress. "He can't come home tomorrow."

"Well, that's what the doctor said."

She led me to the wall calendar, the one featuring a different picture of the royal family each month, and pointed to the following day's date. "This day is *butsumestu*. It would be back luck to bring him home then. Better to wait for a *daian*, an auspicious day."

The best day for Kei to be discharged, according to my calendar and my mother-in-law, was three days later—an agony of hours. I couldn't wait that long.

"It's just superstition," I couldn't help saying.

Her eyes went dark.

"I'm bringing him home tomorrow."

She didn't like it, but she decided to go along with me, muttering under her breath all the while.

That night after I came home from the hospital, she came to my room with a box.

"I bought this for Kei," she said. "To wear when he comes home from the hospital."

I lifted the lid. Inside was a white gown, dripping with ribbons.

She also produced a basket upholstered with cushions and a quilt featuring a teddy bear motif. I imagined my son, a little pasha, borne out in style.

The next morning we went together, my mother-in-law, Yusuke and I. Okaasan waited at the entrance of the NICU in her pumps and suit, nervously fondling her handbag. Yusuke and I went through the doors, scrubbed and donned gowns and masks. He gave my shoulder a squeeze. "Are you ready?"

The nurses hovered while we slipped Kei's hospital gown off his tiny limbs and dressed him in the gown. They seemed sad to see him go. One of them even wiped her eyes as we settled him in the basket.

"*O-sewa-ni narimashita*," Yusuke said with a deep bow.

The doctors and nurses bowed in turn and wished our boy good health.

Yusuke carried the basket as we made our way out of the NICU for the last time. Almost as soon as we stepped through the doors, Okaasan swooped down and lifted Kei out of the basket. She carried him in her arms to the elevator, down to the parking lot, and to the car, Yusuke beside her. I stumbled along behind, trying to keep up.

• • • • •

I've never seen any of Georgia O'Keefe's portraits, but she first drew attention with her sketches of people.

When she was teaching at Columbia College in South Carolina, she painted a portrait of one of the professor's daughters and gave it to him as a gift. She loved children. She wanted desperately to become a mother, but Stieglitz was opposed. He wanted to protect her pure artistic spirit. He thought that a baby would distract her. And anyway, he had grown children of his own.

Maybe he was right about Georgia. If she'd gotten pregnant, the world might have been deprived of her sensual flowers, her desert skulls. And then maybe I wouldn't have been inspired to paint the dappled sea and the spiky black pines of Japan. I loved the image of her, Georgia, a strong woman in a white dress, backed by endless sand. I imagined her against a stormy sky, cacti blooming at her feet, so far from home (she was born in Sun Prairie, Wisconsin).

She wanted to have babies, but Alfred Steiglitz, the one who ran the studio, the one who showed her work on his walls and took those famous pictures of her said, "No." So she painted.

When Kei was born, I suddenly lost all interest in art. He was my best creation, and no pen or brush could ever come close to the perfection of his skin, soft as rain. His fat cheeks, drooping. The downy hair. And then there was the smell of him, the sweetness of his scalp, the damp milky breath, the clean sweat.

Once I had been able to stand before paintings in lengthy contemplation, but now I wanted to look at nothing but my beautiful boy.

For the first few weeks after he was born, after he was released from the incubator and into my arms, I was with him constantly. I carried him against my heart in a pouch, nursing him every couple of hours. I didn't let him out of my sight until one Saturday afternoon, two months after his birth, my mother-in-law suggested that I needed a break.

"Why don't you go for a walk or something?" She said, her voice filled with honey. "Every mother needs a break from time to time. Yusuke and I are here. He'll be fine."

I weighed her offer for a moment, reluctant to leave Kei, but then I offered a wavery smile and unstrapped him from my body.

Yusuke's mother took him into her arms and saw me off at the door.

I stumbled into the sunlight, unaccustomed to being unencumbered. After a few tentative steps, I set off on a stroll.

The world looked different since Kei had been born. A dragonfly darted past me and I thought about how, in a few months, he would gaze upon the blue-winged thing with wonder. His fingers would stroke the petals of cosmos, blades of grass, puffs of dandelions for the first time ever. I imagined him toddling through this neighborhood, each step an adventure.

By the time I got home, my breasts were heavy with milk. Wet splotches darkened my T-shirt. I tossed off my windbreaker and went in search of Kei.

I found him in the living room. Yusuke was sprawled across the *tatami*, reading the newspaper. My mother-in-law was holding our son, close to her chest, and she was feeding him milk from a bottle.

"What are you doing?" I cried out. "You know that I'm breastfeeding."

She shrugged. "He was hungry. He cried and you weren't here, so I had Yusuke go out and buy some formula."

"You had no right." I snatched the bottle from her hand.

She looked up as if slapped. "I was only trying to help. He's my grandson. My son's son."

Kei started crying then.

She began to rock him, but I scooped him out of her arms and left the room.

# 1997

I TRY TO IMAGINE WHAT IT WOULD BE LIKE TO RELINQUISH THE CARE of one's son to another willingly. As I stir the grits, I look at Veronica, smoking at my kitchen table, and wonder how she had felt when she left her son behind.

"So what is that you're making?" she asks.

"Shrimp and hominy grits. It's good for the soul."

She smirks. She was less than impressed with Spaghetti-Os I served up last time, but I know she'll eat up anyway.

"Ready for another drink?" I ask her.

"Sure." She holds out her empty glass.

We are having watermelon daiquiris. I refill her tumbler with pink sludge. "So how are things going with Shima-san?" I ask.

"Okay," she says, and shrugs.

She's already told me that she's been out to dinner with him. He sends her hibiscuses and *santan*, which Veronica suspects he has imported from the Philippines.

Boxes of cookies from Negros.

"Do you think he'll ask you to marry him?"

She sighs and looks out the window, past the palm trees, past the sun-bleached sand, to the horizon. "He's asked me already. He says that Luis can come and live with us. My mother, too."

I know that she doesn't love this guy. She isn't even attracted to him. And yet I know that she will go ahead and marry him.

110

"Maybe you'll meet someone else," I say.

She shakes her head, swinging her curtain of hair. "I miss Luis. I don't want to wait any longer. And I'm tired of the Cha Cha Club."

All this talk has unsettled my stomach. I feel the flutter of nervousness when I should be getting hungry. The grits are starting to congeal in the pan.

Veronica shrugs and gestures to the table set with paper plates. "Let's eat," she says. There is nothing else to do.

• • • • •

The sky's purpling in the south. I flick on the TV to see what's happening. There's a big white swirl in the blue of the ocean. A typhoon is heading this way.

The satellite image gives way to scenes of rain pelting the streets of Nagasaki. A woman in high heels darts between puddles, her pink umbrella suddenly inverted by a blast of wind. This is followed by the requisite shots of stranded passengers, the notice boards listing cancelled ferries and flights.

On the weather map, the storm looked large, but I'm not frightened. I no longer bother to tie down my possessions or bolster the windows. I open the window and catch the wind in my face. "I dare you!" I shout.

Already the glass is beginning to rattle in its panes.

I check for candles and wine. Cigarettes. And then I wait.

The typhoon arrives a few hours later. Having had a few glasses of Merlot, I'm warm as toast. I feel like flirting with the roaring beast outside.

The door resists my push, but I manage to open it. And then I'm outside, wet to the bone in an instant. I can see flying carpets and whiplashed trees.

The people who die in typhoons around here are the ones who are stupid enough to go out in them. You read about people getting hit by airborne debris, or cars washed off the road.

I don't think I'm stupid, standing here. I just want to feel the sting of the rain on my skin, the assault of the wind. I want to be reminded that I am a force of nature.

After a few minutes, I go back inside, sop up the puddles, and take a hot bath.

In the morning, the sky is pure blue, no sign of fleece. But there's still enough wind to keep the waves churning.

I jump into my bathing suit and a layer of clothing and then I head to the beach. Already, at seven a.m., there are surfers out on the waves. Eric is surely among them.

When I spot him, I'm standing at the edge of the beach, letting salt water slosh over my sneakers. He's gliding toward me, graceful as ballet. I watch as he hops off the board and turns back to the horizon, already scouting his next ride. I could call out to him, but I don't. I wait till he notices me.

"You're up early," he says. And then, seeing my face, "Is something wrong?"

"Eric." My voice wobbles. It's the first time I've used it today. "I want you to teach me to surf."

He stares at me for a long moment. At first, I think he might laugh, but he moves closer, slings a wet arm over my shoulder, and gazes up the beach. "Hold on a sec. I'll get you a board."

With Eric alongside, I paddle out a hundred yards or so, trying hard not to fall off. I'm pressed against fiberglass, waves pushing me back, threatening to send me to the bottom of the sea. In the hiss of the surf, I hear words: "You're too old for this. Your body's been ravaged by cigarettes and booze and grief. Get back on the sand where you belong."

But what would I do there? Sketch? I don't want to paint this sea anymore. Not the beach, not the surfers, not the black pines shading the parking lot. I want to immerse myself in water, to become new, pure. With virtue restored, I will be able to get my boy back. At least that's what I'm telling myself as I spit out yet another mouthful of brine.

I turn my head, gather my breath and shout to Eric.

"What?"

"I said I don't think I can do this. I'm out of shape."

He smirks. "Sure you can. Just a few more yards."

And so I dig my arms into the water again, muscles screaming in protest. He was right, I think. Yoga would have been better.

Finally, thoroughly winded, I'm allowed to stop paddling.

"Now we're just going to ride back to shore," Eric says. He isn't breathing hard at all.

I let my cheek fall against the board and cling to it like a shipwreck victim. The water rocks me, the board bobs and sways.

"Here comes a big one," Eric says, looking over his shoulder. "Try not to fall off, okay?"

I can feel the wave spitting on my shoulders and then it lifts me and carries me forward. And then it dumps me into a sand bar, and I find myself picking seaweed out of my hair.

"Alright, get up," Eric says. "Let's try it again."

• • • • •

I make a date with Eric to go shopping. He picks me up at my apartment and takes me to a little shop called Surf Bob. Its shutters are down and its front door locked even though according to the sign out front it should be open by now.

"Out of business?" I suggest.

Eric shrugs. "Naw, the owner just lives on *Awa Jikan*—Tokushima Time."

Ah, yes. Southern laziness.

"Let's go have a cup of coffee." I nod toward the cafe next door and we go in. Except for a pony-tailed guy reading a phone-directory-sized comic book, the place is dead.

The proprietor spends a few seconds wiping the counter before finally sidling over to take our order. I suppose he's on *Awa Jikan*, too.

Eric keeps one eye out the window, watching for Bob or Kenji or whoever runs the place next door. I can tell he's excited about our expedition. He's been filling my ears with talk about guns, thrusters and twinzers all morning. I have no idea what he's saying and I've mostly tuned it out. I expect that I'll know the right board when I see it. I don't need anything too fancy.

"I'll be happy if it simply floats," I say.

But Eric ignores me. He starts telling me the love story of him and his first longboard, a Liquid Shredder with aircraft quality vinyl covering and a Peruvian hardwood stringer. "Man, she was so sweet," he says, and he grabs my hand. "I took her to Hawaii and we went down the face of the biggest wave I've ever seen, under the lip. . . ."

I take a sip of my coffee, and then another, and then an aloha shirt flashes by the window and Eric is yanking me out of my seat and through the door.

He slaps palms with the sleepy-eyed guy fiddling with the lock at Surf Bob. Finally, the key wiggles into place, and we all go inside.

The place smells musty, like it hasn't been aired in a few days. Merchandise takes up every available space. A couple of boards are suspended from the ceiling. Others are fitted into racks on the wall. I stand mute while Taro (what about Bob?), introduces his wares—longboards, skim boards, kneeboards, Hula Girl, Chillybean, Five Daughters, Furcat Epoxy.

My eyes start to glaze. "I want something basic."

Taro nods. "How tall are you?" He doesn't wait for my answer, just measures with his hands, then goes into the depths of his shop and comes back with a hot pink boogie board.

I sigh and shake my head.

"Listen," I say to Eric, "I don't mean to be rude, but this place is making me feel claustrophobic. Can we step outside for a moment?"

Eric nods and guides me out the back door, careful not to bump anything. One nudge and a whole row of nose riders might topple over.

Taro follows us. He magically produces three cold cans of Pocari Sweat. We stand under a black pine and down our drinks.

"Hey, what's that?" I suddenly spot a slab of fiberglass leaning against the back of the building. Its finish is about worn off and a few nicks and gouges mar its surface.

Taro follows my gaze. "Somebody threw it out. I found it on garbage day. I thought I might be able to fix it up."

"How much?" I ask.

Eric loops his index finger around his temple, indicating that I'm crazy. But I like the idea of a seasoned board, a ride with history. "What can I say? It's got a helluva lot more character than Miss Pinky inside. It's been broken in."

Taro shrugs. "You can have it cheap. I can even sell you the stuff you'll need to repair it."

And so we make a deal.

I try to ignore Eric's disappointment as we strap it onto his car. "Cheer up. She doesn't look like much now, but just you wait. You'll be surprised."

I'll smooth out the surfaces to begin with. After I've learned to stand on it, I'm going to paint it.

• • • • •

I have the night off and not wanting to waste it, I drag myself to the video store. My arms are so sore from that morning's surf session that picking a tape off the shelf is sheer agony. I rent *The Year of Living Dangerously*. Back when I was planning on entering the Peace Corps, this was among my top ten favorite movies. Mel Gibson, young and earnest, and the haughty Sigourney Weaver made Third World living seem romantic. The intensity of that film, the kiss in the rain; all that heat and danger; the crush of humanity in the world's third most populous country. Javanese shadow puppets and the musical bong of bamboo.

I feed the video into my machine, a pre-marriage relic bought on sale at Jusco, and uncork a bottle of Chablis. Philip, I remember, had always been very particular about wine. I wonder if he'd approve of this blonde French stuff mixed with steamy Jakarta.

I sit there against the wall, knees bent, back slouched, watching Sigourney slice through the pool with her beautiful crawl. Mel sweats glamorously. Linda Hunt, as an elfin man, slithers in and out of scenes.

I try to picture myself in that setting. I imagine kissing Philip in the rain. In Jakarta.

The next morning I change my plane reservations. I'm not going to Thailand after all.

● ● ● ● ●

"Snakes," Eric says when I tell him I'm going to Indonesia.

"What?"

"You have to watch out for snakes in the water."

I bite down on a smile. "Who says I'm going to be in the water?"

He flips his wet hair back and arches his body toward the blue sky. He no longer shaves his head. It won't be long, I think, before he slides back into hedonism. "Of course you're going to be in the water. Indonesia is a surfer's paradise. You've got Bali, Sumatra—empty waves in warm water."

I can't even stand on my board yet. I don't see the point in wasting world class waves on my low skills. It would be an insult to the sea. Plus, I'd be the laughing stock of the surfing pilgrims.

Still, I'd love to see the look on Philip's face when I show up with a board under my arm. Look at these new dimensions! You think you know all about me, but you don't.

And then there is the photo, not yet taken, that I will send to Kei—Mom, hanging ten on Bali Hai. Maybe he'd show it to his friends. Brag a little. This vision is enough to get me back into the sea.

Eric comes sloshing in behind me like a tag-along puppy. Water is clearly his medium. I'm beginning to feel as if I've never really known him because I've never been with him in the ocean before this. He seems pure, full of innocent enthusiasm. He is focused.

"Here it comes," he says, lunging past me.

I'm too late to hitch a ride on this wave, so I hang back and watch. All those muscles tensed just right, the sea frothing and fizzing out at my knees.

I spot the next one, and for once, my timing is impeccable. I'm up on my knees just as the water begins to lift and carry me. For the first time, I let go of the edge of the board. "Look, Eric! No hands!" My balance lasts for about five seconds and then I'm tossed over and the board flips and bangs me on the head.

I must black out for a second or two because the next thing I know, Eric is dragging me through the shallows. I dig my toes into the sand bar, and then I'm stumbling along, coughing up salt. When we get to shore, we both fall onto our knees, winded from exertion.

"Whew," I say, when my heart finally calms down. "You saved my life."

Eric looks around at the other surfers, some watching us, some still intent on their sport. "I think you're exaggerating," he says. "The water wasn't all that deep where you went down."

"Do you know what the Chinese say? When someone saves your life, you're forever indebted to them."

He raises his eyebrows.

"I'm your slave now."

For some reason, the idea of it brightens me. I can almost see us settling into cozy domesticity, me cooking and cleaning, while Eric plays with Kei at the hearth.

"Get up," he says. "You've got a nasty bruise. We need to get you to a doctor."

Another guy in tropical print knee-length trunks shows up just then. He's rescued my float-away board.

"*Domo arigato gozaimashita,*" I say.

The guy nods and goes back into the water, a merman without words.

Since I'm walking and lucid, Eric doesn't seem to be in much of a hurry. He allows us to shower and change into dry clothes before strapping our boards to the roof of his car and driving in search of first aid.

"This guy's pretty cool," he says, pulling into the gravel lot of an M.D. "He's really hip to Eastern medicine. He does acupuncture."

I suddenly see myself stuck like a silvery porcupine. "I don't know, Eric. Except for this slight throbbing, I feel fine."

Eric rolls his eyes and shifts into park. "C'mon," he says. "I'll hold your hand if you get scared."

He escorts me into the waiting room where a mechanical waterfall provides a soothing gurgle. As opposed to a fish tank, I guess. The lights are dim, not the usual skin-sallowing fluorescent type, and the cushy sofas are a lovely mauve.

"I feel better just sitting here," I say, but the young woman at the reception desk makes me a little nervous. She's got yellow-dyed hair and a ring through her nose. She's reading manga. This doctor is pretty gutsy to put someone like her on display. Then again, maybe medicine is just a hobby for him. I don't see any other patients in the office. I can't imagine how he makes a living with so little business.

After a few minutes, the receptionist looks up from her comics and calls out my name.

Eric nods encouragement. He stretches out as if he's about to snooze.

I go through the beaded curtain into the consultation room. Dr. Sato looks reassuringly normal—short black hair, thick-framed glasses.

"Your head," he says in English before I can get a word out.

"Yes." Is it really that bad?

He shines a light into my eyes, dresses my wound, and then writes out a prescription. "You have a concussion. Take this if the pain gets too bad. And you'd better not drink alcohol tonight."

Does my reputation precede me?

"Thank you." I wait for the medicine and Eric drives me home.

I'm supposed to work at the Cha Cha Club tonight. Lord knows I need the money. My landlord suddenly decided to hike the rent and then there are all those lawyer's fees.

I put on a knit dress that's meant to show off my new surfing physique, hoping it'll be a distraction from my shiner. But the minute I step in the door, Mama Morita shakes her head.

"What happened?" Betty asks, rushing forward. "Did he beat you?"

He? Could she be referring to the yakuza guy of a few weeks ago?

"I got hit with a surfboard."

"Someone hit you with a surfboard?"

"No, no. It was an accident."

I'm about to explain when Mama-san presses a couple of ten-thousand yen bills into my hand. "If you need this, take it," she says. "But I can't have you in here looking like that."

There are strings attached to this money, indentured servitude if not loan sharks. She's got a heart of gold, but she's also a businesswoman. I take the money anyhow.

"Okay. I'll be back in a few days."

And that's how I wind up alone, not drinking wine, spying on the house where my son lives.

• • • • •

The day I left Yusuke, I lost my home, including the room I'd finally come to feel was mine. To be sure, it took a couple of years before I felt anything other than "guest," and a barely tolerated one at that. But I had squatter's rights. My scent began linger in those rooms, my cells, shucked off, began to accumulate like dust. The pictures I hung on the walls, the residual aroma of the curries and casseroles I cooked, the echoes of my favorite music and the persistent hooks that sometimes even Yusuke hummed—all these were marks of my presence. My spoor.

Against all odds, I grew to love that house with its tiny sequestered rooms: the hole in the floor where we hung out legs in winter while peeling oranges at the *kotatsu*; the tiny garden, walled in by bamboo, that was revealed by the opening of a slid-

119

ing paper door; the alcove which featured a different flower arrangement each week, where the paintings on the wall altered with the seasons. And I loved the deep red wood of the stairs that led to our bedroom, the filigree carved out of the wood, the tree trunk, smooth and bark-less, that held up a corner of the porch awning. The carefully selected stones paved in the bathing area floor.

There were times when I found myself missing all that, when I wanted to torch my thin-walled apartment. But these thoughts were meant only to distract myself from what I had truly lost.

After dark there are a few good citizens wandering the streets with their dogs or their cigarettes. There are even some decked out in slippery track suits, pumping their arms as they race-walk in the moonlight. In the dark, no one notices me much. I try to move with purpose. It's a cross between loitering and pacing. Sometimes, if I see a stranger approaching, I glance at my watch and then look up the road. I cross my arms and tap my foot. When the stranger passes, I fix my attention on the house again.

At nine p.m. there's a light on in the kitchen, another glowing in the living room. The windows are open, the sliding paper doors pushed back so the house can suck up fresh air. My former mother-in-law blames air-conditioning for any number of ills and she'd rather sit veneered with sweat than find comfort in artificial weather.

At any rate, her tolerance for humidity allows me to see the back of my son's head as he sits in front of the TV. I can't make out what he's watching. Hopefully, Obaasan is monitoring his viewing habits and he's enraptured by a program on wild animals or the workings of the human body as opposed to some cop show.

I can't see what Kei is watching, but I can see the way the flickers of light fall on his hair. I watch just that for a long time.

When I check the time again, it's after ten and Kei is still watching TV. Doesn't she know that it's past his bedtime? How can she let him stay up so late when he has school in the morning? Maybe I should make an anonymous phone call.

Yusuke's still out, probably wining and dining (mostly the former) clients or, and this makes my stomach twist, bouncing around on a bed in some love hotel with his new girlfriend.

By this time, my bladder is fixing to burst, so I decide to take a little stroll and find a spot to relieve myself. I take my time, meaning to ration out my energy, make it last till morning, and then return to my vigil.

The porch light is now on, but the rest of the house is dark.

I know where he is sleeping. He has that middle room on the second floor. A twin bed. A dartboard hung on the back of the door. Maya has brought these details to me, but I've imagined it all before: the poster of Nakata, a snowglobe from Disneyland.

I'm out there for another hour, swatting mosquitoes and dabbing at my sweaty upper lip with a handkerchief, before I get the courage to try the door.

I try the handle slowly and push my way in. And then I'm standing in the entryway in the dark. I'm holding my breath and I swear I can hear the tick of every clock in the house. Yusuke's mother is snoring.

My heart is slamming around inside me. My head is light. I'm scared enough to faint, but I slip out of my shoes anyway.

In my absence, nothing has changed much. All of the pottery vases are in their original spots. I still know the location of the creaky floorboards.

Just as I put my foot on the bottom stair there's a burst of light through the window. Headlights, I realize. A car engine growls to a stop. Yusuke's home.

I don't care if I wake his mother now. I bolt to the entryway, grab my shoes as Yusuke slams the car door, and let myself out the back way. For the rest of the night, I crouch in the shadows under the carport. I keep my eyes on Kei's window.

At about two a.m. a light goes on in the kitchen. I see Yusuke's mother at the sink. She fills a glass of water from the tap, drinks it, and looks out into the night. Her nightgown drapes unevenly. With one hand, she touches her chest, the ghost flesh. I've seen the scar there. I've touched it myself.

# 1995

I REMEMBER THAT NIGHT WHEN YUSUKE AND I SAT IN THE DOCTOR'S office. Kei slept across my lap, his temple sweating against my forearm. I shifted his weight and tried to tune in to the doctor's words. There were many technical terms that I couldn't make out, but I understood "*gan*" (cancer) and "*shujutsu*" (surgery).

I watched Yusuke's face, gauging the seriousness of the disease in the tightness of his jaw. His eyes were dry. He nodded slowly and thoughtfully. He seemed to have hope.

But what if she died? What did Confucius say about orphans? Was a son then tied to his parents' graves? I knew that my mother-in-law believed her husband's spirit would get angry if she didn't put out green tea for him every morning, or light a cigarette and leave it smoldering at the family altar, like a stick of incense.

Yusuke had always shrugged off these practices as superstition, though he still knelt at the altar in the mornings and chanted a sutra.

I did none of these things. It was understood that I, as a foreigner, did not believe. My heresy was politely ignored. I wondered if Okaasan would pray to her dead husband when she found out that she had cancer.

But then, after we bowed our way out of the doctor's office, Kei, now draped over Yusuke's shoulder, he said, "Don't tell my mother about the cancer, okay? We'll just say that it was benign."

My jaw dropped. "Why?"

If I knew my days were numbered, I'd hop on a plane bound for Tanzania. I'd visit all the museums I hadn't yet gotten to. I'd eat chocolate cake whenever I wanted and splurge on massages and manicures. Or, I might try to cure myself.

"If we tell her, she might lose hope. She must retain her vitality. She must be strong."

I didn't agree, but I nodded. "Okay. I won't say a word."

He got us settled in the car, then went back to check on his mother in her room.

I am loathe to admit this, but I imagined her dead, us free. I tried to feel sad, but sorrow is heavy and I was suddenly light.

• • • • •

A few days before the operation, we took Yusuke's mother to the hospital and helped her settle in. Until the surgery, she was assigned to a ward with three other patients. They all stared at me, the foreigner, curiosity beating out politeness. I probably would have stared, too. There wasn't much to do in that room. A coin-operated TV sat on a table next to each bed. The window afforded a view of the parking lot. The other women had been in the hospital for weeks and there was no one sitting at their bedsides.

My mother-in-law made a grand entrance. She stood in the doorway, the only one with make-up and styled hair, and announced her name. And then she begged everyone's cooperation and tolerance: "*Yoroshiku onegai shimasu.*"

"This is my son," she said gesturing to Yusuke.

He bowed and mumbled his own greeting.

She didn't bother to mention me.

I decided to cut her some slack. She was a sick woman, after all. And these other patients would find out soon enough who I was. I'd promised Yusuke that I'd take care of her, in the same way she had taken care of me when I was in the hospital.

Okaasan sat down on the edge of the bed, her spine straight.

Her feet dangled a few inches from the floor. Her hands lay in her lap, cupped one within the other. She sighed.

"The food here is quite good," I said, wanting to reassure her somehow.

She snorted.

Ah, yes. I was the one who couldn't tell the difference between food cooked on a gas range and food cooked on an electric one, the woman who thought that Thai rice was just as tasty as the Japanese grain. What could I know about food?

A nurse came in then with a pair of pajamas. "Why don't you change into these, Yamashiro-san?"

My mother-in-law sat there for a long moment without acknowledging the nurse. I could tell she was going to be a difficult patient. Finally, the nurse laid the striped pajamas on the bed and strutted out.

The next morning, the day before the operation, I dropped Kei off at the neighbor's house with a pile of his favorite books and toys.

He started wailing as soon as I turned my back. His cries echoed in my head for the rest of the day. I could still hear them as I drove to the hospital, radio blasting, mind scrambling for conversational gambits to carry my mother-in-law and me through the next six hours.

I breezed into her room with a neatly-wrapped parcel—pajamas from home, tangerines, and the long-handled tool she used to beat the stiffness out of her shoulders. I'd included a photo of Kei being silly. I figured the sight of a boy with pants on his head and tongue sticking out would add some much needed levity to the situation.

She grunted when I handed over the bundle, but smiled when she found the picture. She immediately propped it up next to the TV.

I noticed that the lady in the next bed had an oxygen mask cupped over her face, whereas the day before she had been breathing on her own. It must be hard to keep up your spirits, I thought, when everyone around you was dwindling.

"That your little boy?" another patient asked, limping in with her I.V. pole.

"Yes," I said. I was sure that she'd already heard all about me.

"*Kawaii*," she said. "Cute."

I tried to ignore her bald head. I made myself look straight into her eyes when I said, "Thank you."

When the woman had struggled back under the covers and flicked on her TV, Okaasan finally spoke. "What's wrong with me? I want to know."

I froze. I thought we'd talk about the weather or how her orchids were faring. I had two or three anecdotes about her favorite grandson lined up. I wasn't prepared to talk about her diagnosis.

"You should talk to Yusuke," I said. "I didn't understand everything the doctor said."

She sighed. "I did talk to him. A small cyst, he said. Nothing to get excited about. But I know that he's lying."

I turned away so she wouldn't read the truth in my eyes. "I'll make you some tea."

I thought about fleeing. The door was just three feet away. If I made up some excuse—a fever for Kei, a long-distance phone call from my family—maybe I could make a graceful exit. But after I brewed the tea and handed Okaasan her cup, she started to talk about something else.

As it turned out, the day went by quicker than I expected. Visitors came with packets of money and boxes of cakes. I kept busy serving them tea and rounding up folding chairs. The ladies from Okaasan's ikebana class and English conversation circle, and, for half an hour, Yusuke, took care of the small talk.

By the time they'd all left, Okaasan was exhausted and ready for a nap. She slipped into sleep and I just sat there thumbing through magazines, trying to figure out which Japanese celebrity was bedding whom.

• • • • •

After Okaasan had been dressed in blue paper and loaded onto a gurney, after we'd pressed her hand and urged her to be strong, we went into a little room to wait. Other families waited with us. Some had been there for awhile, to judge from the debris of meals. One woman was stretched out on the long vinyl sofa, her head pillowed by a bag of knitting. Her shoes and socks were off, revealing gnarls and corns. She snored softly. With time, I guessed, you could get used to that place, feel just as comfortable as you might in your own bedroom. Worry and grief crowded out shame. When someone you loved was on the table or hooked up to a respirator in the ICU, what you looked like to strangers didn't really matter.

So I didn't worry too much about the streaks of chocolate ice cream on Kei's T-shirt. Yusuke hadn't shaved in a couple of days and his eyes were puffy from too much whiskey the night before, too little sleep.

I'd put on make-up and brushed my hair. My dress spilled smoothly over my hips. I thought that I looked good and that there was something obscene about it. Better if I'd smudged my mascara, wrinkled my clothes.

In the corner, a man was chain-smoking. A young woman fiddled with her cell-phone, in spite of the sign prohibiting satellite calls. She belonged in some nightclub, a booth at Mister Donut's, not this purgatorial chamber.

Yusuke paced and sighed. Kei spent a few minutes studying our companions before he began raiding the bookshelf. Children came here often for last looks at grandparents, for their first lessons in mortality. The kids' books were well worn, thumbed through, some of the covers hanging like one-hinged doors.

Kei found a book about ships and settled on a sofa to "read" it aloud. I watched his rosebud mouth working out words, the thick lashes, the dimples in the backs of his hands. Like always, I got lost in his beauty. Sometimes it made me ache. I wanted to gather him up, the way children embrace teddy bears or favorite blankies. I even wanted to share him a little, knowing that his magic touch could change the atmosphere in that little room. He could make us forget about needles and knives. One little squeeze and all tremors would be gone.

The operation lasted for four hours. When, at last, the surgeon called our name, Yusuke stepped forward and I pulled Kei onto my lap. He was half-asleep by then, having run up and down the stairs more times than I could count. His belly was full of rice balls and bananas.

The surgeon smiled a little and the creases in Yusuke's forehead softened. They bowed to each other and then Yusuke turned to me. "They think they got it all," he said. "I'll go in and see her now."

I nodded. I started rocking Kei to sleep. I didn't want him to see his grandmother in a morphine haze, tubes trickling liquid into her veins. I wanted to keep his world perfect, free of sorrow and disease, for just a little while longer.

When I finally went in to see her, I transferred Kei to his father's arms and went in alone.

She was small against the white sea of a bed. Her eyelids fluttered open. She whispered something. I leaned closer to hear it.

"*Gan, desu yo?*" Cancer, right?

I nodded, not quite sure if she could see me, or if she would even remember this later.

"But you'll be okay," I said. "The doctors got it all out."

Her eyes closed again and she dove back into the twilight zone.

I put my hand on her forehead, the closest I'd ever come to giving her affection.

• • • • •

I wasn't sorry that I'd broken my vow not to tell. She had a right to know. Besides, she'd figured it out on her own. But when I saw the despondency in her eyes two days later, I wondered if she was going to put up a fight or if she had already given up.

She wouldn't eat, said the drugs made her queasy. The hospital gruel went cold and hard.

"C'mon, Yamashiro-san," the nurse said. "If you want us to take out the I.V. you'd better start eating."

She closed her eyes and set her jaw, mad at the world and one foot stepping toward the grave.

The doctor dropped by with good news. "Her blood count is good. The suture is healing nicely." But as soon as the doors had creaked shut, she'd hiss, "*Uso bakkari.*" Lies, all lies.

"Look," I said. "If you want to get better, you have to think positively."

"You don't care what happens to me," she replied. "You're hoping that I die. I know. I was a daughter-in-law once, too."

I brought in balls of rice wrapped around sour plums, green tea cakes, bits of fish—all her favorite things—but she wouldn't take a bite.

Finally, I brought in Kei and propped him on the edge of the bed with a spoon and some pudding.

"Obaachan, say 'ahhh.'" Kei dipped the spoon into the cup and carefully launched it toward her lips.

She kept them pressed tight at first, but who could resist that little boy charm? She cracked a smile and then broke down for a taste.

Kei cooed and clapped. I pretended not to notice that she was giving in.

• • • • •

In the mornings, after Yusuke had left, I lingered over Kei. Sometimes I'd watch him for a full ten minutes before tickling him awake with feather strokes on his soles, soft kisses on his belly. He rolled into my arms, smiling, his eyes still shut.

He was big enough to ride a tricycle, big enough to wash his hands without my help, big enough to answer the phone, even. But I carried him like a baby to his place at the breakfast table. I watched as he woke to scrambled eggs and triangles of buttered toast.

His passion, just then, was dinosaurs. In between bites, he recited a litany of ancient beasts: mastodon, tyrannosaurus rex, brontosaurus, raptor. I asked him questions, just to keep him talking, just to stay a bit longer in the world that most interested him.

"Are brontosauruses carnivores or herbivores?"

"They eat grass," he said in his most professor voice. "Herbivores."

"And how about raptors?"

"Meat."

One look at the clock told me I was running late. I'd miss my mother-in-law's breakfast time if I didn't get on the ball.

Kei was just going next door, to the neighbor's house, but I packed him a lunch and a bag of toys. I tucked a photo of myself in his pocket.

Mrs. Kitagawa wouldn't accept money for babysitting. She gushed about joy and honor every time I brought Kei over, but of course I paid her back. I'd already started tutoring her daughter, Maya, at a cut rate. I was parceling out my slang and colloquialisms at bargain basement prices.

Kei could get dressed by himself, but I slid his pajama bottoms down his legs and pulled off his top, leaving Anpan Man inside out on the floor. My hands skimmed his back and belly, the shoulder bones jutting like angel wings. I breathed him deep before I tugged a T-shirt over his head, helped his hands find the armholes. He had an arm around my neck as he stepped into his pants.

I'd seen him put on his shoes many times before, but as he sat in the entryway, I held his foot in my hand and guided it into a sneaker. Then the other one.

"Why do I have to go to Maya's house?" he asked, eyes dark, like it was a punishment.

"Because Obaachan is in the hospital. You know."

"Why can't I go with you? You said I make her happy. I can feed her." He tugged on my arm. "I can help you."

Yes, every time he entered the ward, she softened. She tried harder. But it was not Kei's job to make her well. That was asking too much. He was only four years old.

"Obaachan gets tired easily. She needs to rest and there's nothing for you to do while she's sleeping."

He drooped. Kicked at the floor.

"Hey," I said, tilting his face up to mine. "I'll miss you. A lot."

• • • • •

I spent that day, and the days that followed with Okaasan, fetching drinks, boxes of tissues, and doing her laundry. I hummed along as she ran through her daily complaints, hovered while she took her medicine, and drew the curtains around her bed when she wanted to take a nap.

In the evenings, Yusuke took my place. We exchanged only a few phrases each day. That is, until one night when he burst into the room where I lay sleeping with Kei.

"Jill!"

I forced my eyes open and glanced at the illuminated numerals on the alarm clock. It was well after midnight. Visiting hours at the hospital ended at eight, but Yusuke often stayed later, especially when his mother couldn't sleep.

"Why did you tell my mother she has cancer?"

I saw his hands, curled in fists at his sides. I put a finger to my lips and nodded at our sleeping child, and then I joined him in the harsh hall light.

"I didn't tell her," I whispered. "She guessed it herself."

He shook his head. "You confirmed it. You could have told her that she was wrong."

"She's not a child," I said, my own voice rising. "She has a right to know."

He laughed—one short, sharp bark. "She thinks she's going to die. She's depressed. She's not even trying to get well."

131

"I'm sorry," I said, even though I wasn't.

"Sorry. Ha. A lot of good that does." He stormed down the stairs and out of the house. In the morning, he was still not there.

I brought Kei to the hospital that day for a few hours. He and his grandmother put a puzzle together. She drew pictures for him on a yellow legal pad. I sat in the corner, barely noticed.

Okaasan got better. A few months later, the doctor declared that she was in remission. She wouldn't be dying anytime soon. Not of cancer.

• • • • •

After she came home from the hospital, Okaasan reverted to her role as the queen. I was Cinderella at midnight, ball over. Back on my hands and knees with a bucket of soapy water.

"Take good care of Mother," Yusuke said every morning as he left the house for work. "And don't let her get upset about anything."

In his presence, she was sugar-sweet, clinging to him with a frail claw. But as soon as he'd gone, she became a whiner.

"Look at all the dust balls in the corners," she'd say. Or, "Please! That vacuum is giving me a headache. Can't you just wipe the floor with a wet cloth?"

It felt as if she were punishing me, but for what? For diverting her son's attention for a brief space of time? For not being obsequious?

On some days, I could tune her out, but on others, she dragged my spirit down. I escaped from her in books and videos. I sought refuge with my boy.

One afternoon, he was climbing on the jungle gym in the park while I watched from a bench. His agility astounded me. His grace and confidence.

"Monkey boy," I said.

He hooked his legs over the bars, made scratching-head motions and chittered. "Kee kee." Some little rocks fell out of his pants pocket as he flipped over into a standing motion.

"Mommy," he said suddenly. "Why don't you like Obaachan?"

I froze, unable to form a single word. Yet, he waited for my answer.

"We're different," I replied after a long pause. "We like to eat different things and we have different ideas, so sometimes it's hard for us to live together. That's all."

He started climbing again, but slowly. "Because you're American."

"Well, yes." I wanted to keep things simple. "That's part of it."

He worked his way to the top of the structure, like a spider navigating its web. "What about Otousan? He's not American."

"We're different, too." I felt a sudden chill. The sun was edging down, but there was more to it than that.

I decided to change the subject. "C'mon, Kei. Let's go home now. You can help me make curry and rice."

He scrambled down quickly and jumped to my side. "Will you let me peel the carrots?"

"The potatoes, too."

We ambled along, bumping each other, not talking. I was a little frightened of what I might reveal to him. For weeks I'd been feeling so vague, but he'd been paying attention to everything.

● ● ● ● ●

That day at the playground. That wasn't my moment of truth. In fact, there was never an epiphany, no flash of lightning. I think of it more as a gas morphing into something solid. Gray, finally deepening to black.

A few weeks later, we were sitting around the table, the remains of dinner before us, peeling tangerines for dessert. At some point, Kei had crawled onto my lap and snuggled there still. His grandmother couldn't help but frown at us.

"Aren't you too big for that?" she asked.

Kei ignored her. I'd explained before that Obaachan wasn't used to kissing and hugging, that she had other ways of showing her affection. Not that Kei wasn't aware of it. She indulged him at every turn. But the physical, that was somewhat repulsive to her.

"You know," she went on, "I was thinking that it's time for Kei to start preschool. He needs to make some friends."

My arms tightened around my son. He snuggled closer. "He has friends," I said. "He plays with other little boys at the park."

It was kind of a lie. A lot of times, we were the only ones there. And Kei was too shy to approach other kids, who were in turn put off by the pale-skinned foreign woman who always hovered near-by.

"Think of all the free time you'd have," Yusuke piped in. He had a tendency to frown at us, too. "You could start painting again."

I didn't even want to paint and I didn't think that I could bear to be separated from my boy. But I knew that what they said was true. He needed some rough-and-tumble play with boys his own age. They'd give him vocabulary, teach him how to get along, things I never could. He'd learn to share, for Pete's sake. In this house, he was pampered beyond belief, a little prince with a new toy every hour, snacks behind my back, new shoes as soon as the old ones showed their first scuff.

"Alright," I said. I was afraid to say more. My throat was already clenching.

"There's a fine kindergarten just a little ways from here," Mother-in-law went on in an overly solicitous tone. It was as if she were trying to talk a child into parting from a favorite blankie. "I'm sure you've seen all the little girls and boys in their uniforms."

Yes. I had. They looked like little soldiers—navy blue, when they should have been wearing rainbow shades, ice cream colors. I hated those little brass-buttoned jackets.

"I know someone who was once principal there," Mother-in-law winked. "I'm sure Kei would pass the interview with flying colors."

It sickened me, this competitiveness, this back-door business. Even that—a recommendation from Okaasan's "connection"— would sully my sweet boy's innocence. He was perfect. He didn't need help getting into some fancy preschool.

• • • • •

"You'd better wear a suit," Mother-in-law said, taking in my turtleneck knit dress.

I'd put on lipstick. I figured I was way overdressed for a visit to a kindergarten, but Yusuke's mother seemed to disagree.

Ridiculous. But there were codes to honor, so I marched back up the stairs and threw open the closet door. Artists didn't wear suits much. Neither did stay-at-home mothers. I had a mourning suit, bought for the ceremonies commemorating the anniversaries of my father-in-law's death. It hung at the back, still smelling of incense. I also had a little going-out ensemble made of navy moiré. Totally inappropriate. Was I going to have to borrow something from her?

I went back downstairs. She was still kneeling at the *kotatsu*, perusing the newspaper inserts.

"I don't have a good suit to wear," I said. "I have a black one and a shiny one. I'm wearing this dress."

Her nostrils flared ever so slightly.

"You could go shopping," she said, after a moment. "I'll give you some money. We'll reschedule the interview for tomorrow."

I shook my head. "That won't be necessary." Switching to English, I called up the stairs for Kei.

He came rampaging down in a sweater and corduroys.

"Can't you dress him up a bit more?" Mother-in-law complained. "He's got a little neck tie. And that lovely jacket I bought for him at Sogo."

"He's interviewing for a slot in a preschool, not a job at Sony," I said.

She sniffed and gave me a pity-filled look. Ah, the poor dumb American, she must have been thinking.

Well, so be it. If getting into Rainbow Kindergarten required kowtowing and formal wear, it wasn't the place for my son. And, yeah, maybe I was trying to sabotage the whole thing because I wanted to keep Kei with me. But no such luck.

Kei walked into the teacher's room, bowed and said, "*Ohayo gozaimasu.*"

The staff laughed and clapped. They loved him from the first moment they laid eyes on him.

• • • • •

On the first Monday in April, the Rhythm Room was filled with metal folding chairs. Fifty mothers perched on the edges of the chairs, craning forward with their digital cameras and video recorders. Some of the women were trussed up in kimono. They shuffled across the floor in vinyl slippers, breath impeded by stiff silk. I watched one of them maneuver herself into a folding chair. Then I realized I was holding my breath in sympathy and crossed my legs. The younger mothers and the ones with highlights—hair streaked with magenta or dyed yellow—tended toward suits. Hanae Mori, Chanel, Comme des Garcons. Everyone was wearing make-up. The scent of hair spray was nearly suffocating.

I was so caught up in the pageantry of the mothers that I barely noticed the entrance of the children. A woman at the right of the stage began banging on a piano—some march that seemed vaguely familiar. The children moved forward in two straight lines, one little boy goose-stepping, another pausing to deliver a raspberry to the little girl next to him. She recoiled from the spit spray, then started to cry.

Kei was in the middle. He marched to the beat, eyes straight ahead. I was hoping he'd wave, at least look around for me, but he'd been trained well.

The woman next to me began to sniffle into an embroidered handkerchief. My heart was beginning to feel heavy, too. Was Kei going to turn into some kind of automaton? I had an impulse to

136

drag him out of formation and into a park. Fresh air, open space, room to run.

But once Kei was on stage, I saw his eyes moving. He spotted me and smiled.

Okay. Maybe it wouldn't be so bad after all.

• • • • •

The first morning, with Kei out of the house, the clocks ticked louder. The shuffling of my mother-in-law's slippered feet was like sandpaper rubbing on raw nerves. I'd never noticed how dark and gloomy the corners were.

I spent a good hour sitting down and standing and sitting again. I moved from room to room, trailing my fingers along the walls. I felt like a lovelorn teenager. Unbidden, I joined Okaasan for her morning tea break.

"I wonder what he's doing now," I murmured. A few stray tea leaves swirled in my cup.

Okaasan took a loud slurp. "Why don't you go paint or something?"

I shrugged. Painting was the last thing on my mind.

My mother-in-law leaned forward, a glint in her eyes. "Why don't you have another baby?"

Another baby? How could I love any other child, now that I had Kei? And besides, wouldn't that one grow up and go off to school as well?

I pushed the tea cup across the table. "I think I'll go for a walk. The cherry blossoms are lovely."

She nodded sagely, and let me go.

I slipped into loafers and wandered until my feet were sore, trying to eke some joy from the frothy petals that fluttered in the breeze. But the stone on my heart didn't budge until I saw Kei at the gate and enfolded him in my arms.

I thought it would get easier as the weeks went by, that I would learn to fill my days and to rejoice over Kei's ever-expanding world. He brought home new words, messy craft projects, small gifts from new friends. When he talked about his teacher, I saw the signs of a crush. I was jealous.

The house seemed darker with each day, my mother-in-law's presence more suffocating.

One late morning, I poured myself a glass of wine and the day became softer. I downed another, and took a nap. When I woke up, I found Kei in the kitchen, eating rice crackers with his grandmother.

"Oh, baby. I'm so sorry. You should have woken me."

Kei smiled. He didn't seem to be bothered. He handed me a tube of construction paper. I unrolled it.

"I drew a picture of you, Mommy. Do you like it?"

I saw a wobbly circle, three hairs sprouting out on top. Smudged eyes. "I love it."

• • • • •

On my birthday, Kei stayed home with his grandmother and Yusuke took me out for *kaiseki ryori*. We knelt on cushions at a low table in a private room. The door slid soundlessly open, and a bowing waitress placed exquisitely prepared tidbits before us— sugared beans threaded onto pine needles, tiny terrines, bites of fish adorned with yellow chrysanthemums. I followed Yusuke's lead, admiring each dish, each morsel before popping it into my mouth. The waitress stepped away, as quietly as a cat, and reappeared with more dishes.

We were so busy eating and admiring, guessing at ingredients, pouring sake, that we were halfway through the meal before either of us ventured conversation.

"How is work going?" I asked.

Yusuke shrugged. "Busy. How's your painting?"

"You know that I haven't been painting."

"Maybe you should."

I sighed. "I'm blocked. Maybe if I had my own studio…" What I wanted was to get out of that house, to someplace we could call our own.

Yusuke reached under the table and pulled out a small black box. It was tied shut with a silvery ribbon.

"What's this?" I asked. I thought earrings. Diamonds, maybe.

"Happy birthday." He went back to eating, didn't even look at my face.

I tugged at the ribbon and let it fall to the table. Inside the box, nestled on a bed of cotton, was a polishcd kcy. House key, I thought, and my heart beat a little faster.

"It's for the gallery," Yusuke said. "You can do whatever you want with it. Turn it into a studio, have shows, throw parties..."

I just looked at it, laying against the cotton. I didn't want to touch it. "What about you? The gallery is important to you." It was also something that bound us, our mutual love of art.

"We've got projects lined up for the next five years. I don't have time to hold art shows, but it would be a shame to let that space go to waste. Art is more your thing anyhow. And you're bored, right?"

I put the lid back on the box. "Thank you," I said. When the waitress brought the next course, I had no appetite.

• • • • •

One day, as Kei and I walked home from nursery school, we paused at a construction site. Kei peered up at the men in pantaloons, perched on the scaffolding with hammers and cigarettes.

"What are they making?" he asked.

"A house." I could tell from the frame that it would be large and airy. The wood smelled fresh. I closed my eyes and breathed in deeply.

I imagined Yusuke, Kei and I moving into this house, my son playing in the yard. A small park with a swingset and slide and drinking fountain was just a hundred yards away. We could start again here, initiating brand new customs. We could be happy.

As we sauntered the rest of the way home, Kei singing a song about tulips, I completed the house in my mind. I shingled the roof and painted the walls a cool blue, put furniture in every room.

That night when Yusuke came home, I told him what I'd conjured.

It was ten-thirty and he was just sitting down to the supper I'd prepared hours before—meat, a little dry from being micro-waved, and a bowl of steaming rice. I poured him a glass of beer and then another.

"I don't think I can live with your mother any longer," I said, looking at the table. I studied the nicks and scratches there, not wanting to see his face.

I heard him swallow, chew, then swallow again.

I lifted my gaze. "Please, let's live somewhere else. It would be better for everyone."

He took another swig of beer before answering. "This is our house. My mother is part of our family. If you don't like it, go back to America."

He was bluffing wasn't he? Or he thought that I was. He couldn't have possibly meant that he would be indifferent to my departure, that he would choose her over me.

I decided that I would bring it up another time. For all I knew, there had been trouble at work—a crack in a foundation, a fight among carpenters, someone pushing for a pay raise. He didn't talk about work with me. He didn't think I would understand. He didn't really talk to me about anything at all anymore.

• • • • •

I'd always taken Philip for a bridge-burner. (Remember what happened to Lilah, the ex-girlfriend who was dumped without even a phone call.) But I'd hoped that I'd stick in his brain, jab at his conscience from time to time, if nothing else. I'd treated him well. I'd been devoted to him, and sooner or later, he'd wind up with someone who'd break his heart. And then he'd feel sorry for abandoning me.

Still, I was a little surprised when the letter arrived. My moth-er forwarded it to me in Japan. There was no return address, so she didn't know who it was from, but I recognized the handwriting. It was postmarked Hollywood.

I took it up to my room where I'd be able to read it alone, away from Okaasan. I wasn't sure how I'd feel and I was a little scared of having the past rear its head. I unfolded the typed pages slowly, took note of the Fox Studios letterhead.

Dear Jill,

It's a very strange feeling to put finger to keyboard and write to you after all this time, but I thought it was high time to reinitiate contact. It's not often that one meets truly good people in the world, and it's important to maintain ties with those people throughout one's life. I still keep in touch with friends in France, Senegal, Sierra Leone, Myrtle Beach, Columbia, etc. Anyway, you're someone I don't want to stop knowing. I love counting among my friends people who have the balls to go places where they have no friends or relatives and manage to make a life for themselves against the odds for most people. Like you.

To the average person, the whole concept of this letter is a bit weird. I just couldn't come to grips with knowing that you're somewhere on this planet and not saying, "Hey, you're a good person, and there's no reason we can't be friends.' If only 'cause we've seen a whole lot more since Columbia. I knew it would be okay to talk, and I think letters in a general sense are pretty healthy.

My living situation is a bit different these days. I'm living with a woman I met in Senegal. Her name is Jennifer. I think you'd like her. She's writing a screenplay and I'm working in TV here in El Lay, but I'm trying to get over to Europe to get a head start

141

on what will soon be a commercial onslaught in my field of interest. Jennifer and I have been together for quite awhile, but haven't gotten around to the "M" word. I have a couple of friends who have recently married and seeing them scares the hell out of me; some of their dreams are truly dead. I just know that with such a big world, I won't believe any of it until I see it first-hand. Any enlightenment is appreciated.

So this is how it ends.

I'd love to hear any anecdotes you might have about Japanese baseball. Please tell your Japanese friends that Shonen Knife is a cult phenomenon that is destined to break out massively any day now.

Philip

After I finished the letter, I sat there on the *tatami*, for a long moment, my heart banging like a drum. My life was contained in that town, that house. I had no car, not even a driver's license. When I thought of Japan, I saw a narrow string of islands stranded in the Pacific Ocean. And the island where I lived, Shikoku, was separate from the rest—the bustling international cities of Honshu, the bullet train zipping past Mt. Fuji. There wasn't even a bridge connecting Shikoku to the modern world.

Islanders take isolation for granted, but I'd originally come here, in part, to stretch my boundaries. I'd thought my world was expanding, but now I was an *oku-san*—a woman of the interior.

When door-to-door salesmen came around, that's what they called me: "*Okusan!* Wife!" Sometimes, they called me "Mother!" But I wanted to be known by some other name. I just wasn't sure what.

I held the paper tight, imagining that it was a ticket of some kind. But as many times as I read Philip's words, I could detect no invitation, no encouragement. If I was going somewhere, it would be on my own.

• • • • •

For a few weeks, I waited. I charted out the most auspicious days on the calendar and I picked one. While Yusuke was at work and Okaasan was at her *ikebana* lesson, I packed a bag for Kei and another for myself and checked into a hotel. I admit that I hadn't planned very far ahead. I figured I'd rent an apartment somewhere and get a job teaching English or art, and Kei would visit his father on the week-ends.

For the first few days, all we did was watch TV. I sat in the hotel chair, twirling knots in my hair, wondering how I was going to pull this off. I remembered sitting in another hotel room the night my mother left my father. My brothers and I sat right up next to the TV, our faces closer to the screen than she ever allowed, while she lay on one of the beds. She stared at the ceiling humming "Plain Gold Ring." We watched the small screen till we were sick of it, and then we brushed our teeth and changed into pajamas without being told. A few days later, we were back in the house and my father was gone.

I hadn't called my mother yet. She'd be willing to take us in, but what I needed just then was freedom. So we were sitting there in the gloom, TV blaring, Kei in just his underpants since it was so hot, me in a T-shirt down to my knees, when there was a knock at the door.

I froze.

Kei looked at the door, at the rattling knob. "Mom?" He was already sick of our exile.

"Shhh."

From the other side of the door: "Jill? Open up. I want to talk to you."

Kei jumped up and went to the door. I could have stopped him, I guess. I just watched him slide the chain back and leap into his father's arms. Rescued.

Yusuke flicked the lights on. "What are you doing in here? Are you sick?"

There were dirty clothes on the floor. The beds hadn't been made. I'd smoked a pack of cigarettes out on the balcony and left the ashes standing in a bowl.

"Look, I'm taking you both home," Yusuke said. "This is ridiculous."

My stomach lurched. "No. I can't go back. I'm sorry, I just can't."

If he'd begged me then, would I have gone with him? If he'd said he loved me, that he couldn't live without me? If he'd suggested counseling or a vacation in Hawaii? But then why didn't I come up with some first aid plan for our marriage? We were both stubborn, I guess, and proud.

Kei was still in his arms.

Yusuke stared at me for a moment, and then he walked out with my son.

I should have run after him, but I was thinking, it's okay, it's only for a little while, till I get back on my feet and beat down these cobwebs in my head. I'd bail out of that little box of a room and set us up somewhere cozy. I'd fix up a room for him with cowboy curtains and an airplane mobile. There would be light streaming through every window, green plants everywhere.

I just needed a little time.

I stood by the window and watched them get into the car. The sudden rev of the engine jolted my heart. In my mind, I could see Yusuke's hands choking the steering wheel, his jaws a vise. Rubber screeched on pavement as he pealed out of the parking lot.

I waited for my heart to settle and my breathing to even out and then I went to the vending machine in the lobby and bought a few cans of beer.

I just needed a little more time.

● ● ● ● ●

When I woke up the next morning, my head was banging. The

overhead light was still on, the curtains drawn. The room smelled like beer and cigarettes—the stink of despair. It had been a long, long time since I'd gotten so drunk. Not since some keg party back in college. I looked around the room, saw the mascara smeared on my pillow, my clothes crumpled on the floor, and was ashamed. All I wanted was to burrow under the covers and wake up from some other dream. It couldn't be real, Kei being gone.

By the time housekeeping came around and rapped on the door, I'd aired the room out a bit and tidied up. The empty aluminum cans had been tossed into the trash along with the ashes and crumpled tissues. I'd taken a shower and changed my clothes. I even made up my face.

I opened the door and nodded to the maid, then eased past her cart of cleaning supplies. When I went to the front desk to check out, the clerk glanced at the space beside me. She must not have been around the night before when Yusuke had taken Kei away. Well, let her wonder. I wasn't about to explain. I slapped down some cash and went out to flag a cab.

At the house, I couldn't bring myself to just open the door and walk inside. I had made a decision. This was no longer my home. I pressed the doorbell.

I looked around for signs of Kei—a nose pressed to the window, a forgotten bucket. I couldn't hear him inside and for a moment, I panicked, thinking that Yusuke might have hidden him away somewhere. Then the door slid open and I saw Okaasan standing there in her white apron, looking vaguely annoyed.

"It wasn't locked," she said. "Why didn't you just come in?"

She turned away before I could answer and I wondered what Yusuke had told her.

"Mommy!" Kei came running down the hall. He threw himself into my arms, nearly toppling me.

I shrugged the bag off my shoulder and gathered him in my arms.

"I want to show you something," he said, lurching toward the corridor. "I drew a dragon."

My muscles froze for a second before I stepped into the house. I set him down and let him lead me to the *tatami* room where his paper and crayons were scattered across a low table.

I knelt beside him. "A blue dragon!" I said.

"See, it's got stripes," he said, pointing to orange slashes.

"It's gorgeous!" How easy it would be to pretend that nothing had happened, that I hadn't left with my bag and passport.

Okaasan brought me a cup of hot green tea on a tray and set it down without a word. "*Arigato,*" I whispered. I lifted the cup, felt the steam on my face. Took a sip. She'd brewed it stronger than usual. Or maybe everything would taste bitter from now on.

"Hey, why didn't you go to school today?" I asked Kei.

He shrugged. "Daddy said it's a holiday."

"Hmm. Did he say anything else?"

He scrunched his forehead. "He said you'd be back tomorrow."

"Well, he was right. But we're not going to stay."

I waited until Yusuke came home. I sat at the table with two glasses and a bottle of whiskey—truth serum. When I heard him come in the door just before eleven, I called him into the kitchen.

"What?" His face was ragged from fatigue. I could tell he'd had a few drinks already.

"We need to talk." I nodded to the chair across from me.

He moved slowly, like someone on the ocean floor, then slouched into the chair. As he loosened his tie, I filled our glasses.

"What?" he said again. That tinge of irritation.

"Yusuke, tell me right now. Do you love me?"

He didn't answer at first. He picked up his glass, swirled the amber liquid around, and took a huge gulp. "What is this about, Jill? Do you have to have romance all the time? Do you want me to buy you some flowers, take you out to dinner?"

That would be nice, I thought, but didn't say. "We don't seem to have much of a relationship," I said, "and I'm trying to figure out what to do about that. So. Do you love me?"

He finished off the glass, then reached for the bottle. "Some things are more important than 'love.'" I swear, I heard the quotation marks. "Duty, for example. Loyalty."

Ah, those Confucian ideals.

"Do you love Kei?"

"Of course."

"But you don't spend time with him."

He sighed. "You don't understand. This is Japan. Things are different here."

It was my turn to take a long swig. "Yusuke, I'm not happy here. I want to go back to the United States."

"You know that's impossible. My mother--"

I put up my hand, blocking his words. My throat was burning from the whiskey. I hadn't even added ice. "Yusuke," I said, suddenly feeling light-headed. "I want a divorce."

The word slammed down like a gate between us. I thought I would fall down. I couldn't tell if I was scared or elated or just buzzed from the liquor. My hands started to tremble, but Yusuke was perfectly composed. He took a nail file from his pocket and started digging grit out of his fingernails.

"If that's what you want."

• • • • •

The lawyer's office looked like my husband's office, or like every other office I'd seen in Japan—big desk, dark paneled walls, black vinyl sofas flanking what my mother would call a coffee table, but was more accurately a place to set down tea cups. On Yusuke's office walls there were paintings. Gotonda-san's walls were bare, save for some official looking documents stamped with orange ink, which I took to be his license. Of course there were no photos of his family around. There wouldn't be.

Gotonda-san stared at me for a moment through his thickly framed glasses. "*Hai?*"

I introduced myself. "I've been told you speak English," I said.

147

He froze.

I decided to rephrase in Japanese. "*Eigo shaberimasu ka?*"

"*Chotto*," he replied. He pinched the air to show me how much he could understand. Only about a centimeter.

I assumed he'd heard all about me from Mama Morita. When I invoked her name, he seemed to remember a few details. He stood up, lit a cigarette, and started nodding vigorously. His glasses slid down his nose. "Sit, sit," he said, waving to the sofa. He laid a yellow legal pad on the table.

"I ask you some questions," he said.

I sat down and tapped out a cigarette of my own.

"Do you work?"

"Yes. I'm a hostess at the Cha Cha Club." No use perjuring myself.

He nodded again several times, pushed his glasses up his nose, and took a drag. The ash on his cigarette was growing perilously long.

"You work at night, yes? So who would be taking care of your son while you were gone?"

"A friend."

"Can you tell me your friend's name?"

"Eric Knudsen."

"He is your lover?"

"No. Just a friend. A fellow American. A male. A celibate yoga instructor, for Pete's sake." Sensing Gotonda-san was beginning to cross to the other side, I took a deep breath and started again. "Although Kei won't be seeing his father as much as before, I will provide strong role models for him."

How American, this guy was probably thinking. As if any judge would give a shit.

Gotonda stared at his notes and sucked his teeth. He drummed the legal pad with his pen.

"Was this Eric your lover before?"

"No."

"You were faithful to Yamashiro-san?"

"Yes. Completely."

I had been an exemplary Japanese wife, had I not? I'd spent six years under the watchful eyes of Okaasan. There was no way she could accuse me of an affair.

I riffled through my past, through my conversations with Yusuke. Had I told him about the post-Phillip Prozac? About the pot I smoked in college? About posing in the nude for the life drawing class?

Was I going to lose custody because I smoked cigarettes?

Gotonda-san puffed his own cigarette and shook his head. "You know," he said, finally looking at me, "It's not a crime in Japan to kidnap your own child."

• • • • •

I called my mother a couple of days after the divorce.

"What do you mean you lost Kei?" she demanded. "What on earth did you do?"

"Nothing."

When she left my father there had never been any question of who would take responsibility for my two brothers and me. Dad was a doctor and he didn't have the time, energy, or inclination to deal with us. He sent money every month, but it was never enough. Remembering her grim mouth in the grocery store check-out line, I wondered sometimes if she'd have preferred not to have to struggle. Maybe she didn't even want to take care of us. But she'd had no choice.

"You must have done something. Did you have an affair?"

I hadn't heard that tone in at least ten years, not since she'd found a joint in my windbreaker pocket. What did I have to do to earn her sympathy?

"I did not have an affair," I said, getting a little bit testy. "If I did anything wrong, it was being born in another country. They won't let me have him because they're afraid that I would take him out of Japan. He's the heir of the house of Yamashiro. The only one."

149

My lack of income and lodging, my desertion—all of those were nothing compared to this fact of heredity. On top of that, the Yamashiro family had connections. I did not. For all I knew, they were paying off the judge.

I could hear my mother's intake of breath, could envision her adjusting the cardigan at her shoulders. "You'll see him on weekends, won't you?" Her reasonable voice. "And during the holidays."

"That'll be up to Yusuke and his mother," I said. "There is no such thing as joint custody in this country."

The silence that followed lasted so long that I thought she'd hung up.

"Mom? Are you there?"

I thought I heard a sniffle.

"Are you telling me, Jill, that I might not be able to see my grandson again?"

I bit down on my lip so hard that I broke the skin. "No, Mom. I'm sure it won't ever come to that."

She paused, considering. "Well, why don't you come home. At least for awhile. It's not good for you to be alone at a time like this."

I remembered long visits to my grandparents' house after my parents' divorce, my mother crying with her sisters while I played Parcheesi with my cousins.

"Thanks, but I need to be near Kei."

I gave her my new address and hung up the phone.

A week later, a package arrived. My mother had sent chocolate chip cookies, which had mostly crumbled in flight, a tattered copy of *My Father's Dragon*, a book I'd read over and over as a child, and a Nina Simone CD.

I cranked up the music, bit into a cookie, and began to read.

# 1997

HERE I AM NOW, ON MY WAY TO THE LAND OF DRAGONS. I'M SITTING in the belly of an Air Garuda 747. I've got my peanuts and my gin-and-tonic and I'm gazing out at the clouds. Sunlight bounces off the wing. My sandals are kicked under the seat in front of me, and I'm thinking about that time Philip set a boom box under my window. It was my birthday. Around midnight. When I heard New Order's "Love Sensation" blasting up from below, I leaned out my window and saw him standing there, in the dark, a dozen red roses in his arms.

I flip through the in-flight magazine and a couple of news-papers, and then I go to the bathroom to check my face. My cheeks are splashed with color, thanks to the sun. My eyes are a little bloodshot, but a few drops of Visine will take care of that. I turn sideways and suck in my gut. The breasts are looking a little droopy, but, hey, I figure he's aged a bit, too.

As we begin our descent, I can hardly contain my excitement. The seat belt suddenly feels like a straitjacket.

A few minutes later, the jet's wheels are bouncing on the tar-mac and the wind screams against the wings. Outside the window I see trees with raggedy leaves, a patchwork of rice paddies. Be-yond, volcanoes.

In spite of my excitement, I'm the last to leave the plane. Last minute doubts nail me to my seat. What if I'm no longer attracted to him? What if I am? And then there is my fear of seeming over-eager. When the aisles have cleared, I stretch my limbs, gather my bags, and deplane.

I see him almost immediately. He's leaning against the wall, and although he is deeply tanned, he's the palest guy in the lobby. He's wearing khaki shorts, a la L.L. Bean, and a T-shirt from the Hard Rock Cafe. Almost ten years on and his wardrobe hasn't changed. His hairline has receded a bit and he's wearing wire rim glasses—something new—but his wiry build remains the same.

He smiles when he spots me and moves forward for a hug. "Hey, big girl. So how ya doin'?"

The honest answer would be, "not so good," but I smile and nod as if everything were hunky-dory. I follow him to baggage claim, trying to keep up with his quick gait and catch all the words he's throwing my way: ". . . right on the beach . . . helluva . . . fucking cannibals . . . you wouldn't believe. . . ."

● ● ● ● ●

I feel as if I've stepped through a time warp. Gone are the years of pining, the resentments and recriminations, the nights of "what if?" We are instantly back into an easy camaraderie, and I can't figure out how I will ever find a way to spill my sad story. There may never be a moment that seems right.

We pick up my bag and my surfboard.

"What the hell is this?" Philip takes a quick look, then launches into a report of the band he saw last week. I don't really get the chance—not then, anyway—to tell him how surfing is saving my life.

We emerge from the airport into thick heat. Smog veils the city beyond. I can smell exhaust fumes and clove and sweat.

As Philip loads my suitcase into the trunk of his car, I edge close to him, checking for a telltale frisson. His bare arm brushes mine, raising goosebumps. Something leaps in my stomach and this brings relief. Already I'm imagining us naked in his bed.

It is raining in Java. The rain pocks the rice paddies, beats out a staccato tune on the roof of Philip's car. It smears across the windshield and is wiped away. Through the gray I can see volcanoes. In the foreground, high-rises loom, upstart affronts to those ancient mountains.

People say that Tokushima drivers are bad, but on these roads there's a kind of free-for-all that I haven't seen yet. Passing is a game of chicken. The cars couldn't be any closer in traffic if they were hitched together.

Philip weaves in and out of lanes, deftly avoiding the beggars who seem inclined to flop across his shiny blue hood, and the *bet-jaks*, the three-wheeled pedi-cabs that remain from Suharto's day and before, to give tourists a taste of colonial privilege.

Philip nearly misses hitting one, and just shakes his head. "These guys..." Third world living has made him blasé.

The city is gray in the rain. I am relieved to enter the mauve and plum of Philip's apartment. I tip the doorman generously and Philip frowns. He doesn't know that I am close to begging myself.

He tosses his keys on the table and pulls off his rain-wet shirt. He is still taut and sinewy. When he raises his arms, I could count his ribs. But I don't. My eyes trail down to his navel, the line of fuzz descending into his shorts.

"A drink?"

It would be impolite to refuse.

"Sure. A glass of wine?"

He pulls a bottle from the refrigerator—an American import that hums soothingly—and grabs two stems. The cork comes out with ease. Not a drop is spilt, each glass filled to exactly the same level. He must do this a lot.

When I reach out for my glass, I notice that my hand is trembling. I notice the rich rose tones.

Philip lifts his glass with one hand, drags a finger across his lower lip with the other. My heart goes giddy-up.

"To reunions," he says, at last.

We chink our glasses together. Real crystal. In my mouth it's all smoke and flowers. My toes start singing. But see, I've built up a resistance. My nerves are on alert.

We're both on the same cushy leather sofa, a thigh's width apart. His knee is bobbing up and down. I want to reach out and make it stop.

But then he's jumping up to put on a CD—how could he forget music?—and the room is suddenly full of cello, the saddest instrument in the world. He doesn't sit back down right away, but goes to the window and pulls back the curtain. "You know," he says, looking out at the rain, "I'm really glad you're here."

My first impulse is to get up and wrap my arms around his waist, but I suppress it and say, "How's your family?"

"Nuala and Nick split up. Did I tell you that?"

"No." I remember admiring them, feeling jealous and hopeful at once.

"Yeah. Nuala decided that she wanted to 'find herself.' She went off to California. Ditched Nick and her five kids."

My head starts to spin. I think I might throw up. I toss back my wine and lean forward to pour another glass. "How could she do that?"

I don't even realize that I've spoken until Philip turns back to me with haunted eyes. "I don't know. But my family, they're like a bunch of lemmings—they supported her, said it was something she had to do." He shakes his head.

I can't listen to any more. "I lost Kei," I say, with my head between my legs.

"What?"

"I had a son," I continue, choking on every word, "and I lost him."

All of a sudden, I'm wailing like a hurricane. More wine is poured. Philip's hands are patting my back, "Hey, hey, it's okay now," as if I'd just had a nightmare. Snot is running down my face. My eyes are burning. I'm thinking that my carefully scripted seduction is shot to hell.

He kisses me. I find it's easier to fuck than to fill in the rest of my story.

• • • • •

It's morning in Jakarta and the aroma of coffee fills the apartment. Sumatran, no doubt. I loll against the pillows in a bed that's big enough for four. Patterned cushions are strewn across the carpet. Otherwise the room is as neat as a pin.

Photos in frames parade across the dresser top: Nuala, Philip's mother, doctor daddy, the twins. Friends don't rate this place of honor. Philip is a family man.

I see no evidence of past flings or current encumbrances: no forgotten lingerie hanging from the closet doorknob, no earrings under the bed, just my own suitcase threatening to spill its contents onto the plush carpet.

The pile is so thick that my feet leave prints. I grab a cotton dressing gown from the back of a chair and pad out into the other room.

"Good morning!" Philip peers out from beneath the stove hood. He's moving a spatula around in a pan. Scrambled eggs. "Did you sleep well?"

"Mmm." I move to the window and try to find ocean. My surfboard sits near the door like a pet waiting to be taken for a walk. All I can see are buildings.

Philip brings me a cup of coffee and kisses the back of my neck. "I know how you need your morning fix," he says. He's shirtless in a sarong. I notice bite marks on his shoulder. Oops.

• • • • •

We eat our breakfast, and then Philip dashes off to work. I go to a bus stop to flag down a ride to the Japanese Embassy. I'm sure Philip would have offered me a lift, but I need to take on this minor challenge by myself. I join the queue under an awning. Behind me, a mother and child share a durian. Its pungency blots out the cologne of the woman in front of me and the spicy ciga-

155

rette of the man in front of her.

All manner of attire can be found on these streets—the sleek three-piece suits of businessmen, both Western and native, T-shirts with skewed English paired with Levis, sarongs, and the head coverings of devout Muslim women. I have dressed conservatively in a plain shirtwaist. Even though it's steamy hot, I'm wearing nylons. I don't want to give the Japanese authorities any reason to deny my visa.

After several minutes, a bus, plastered with an advertisement for a soft drink, chugs up to the stop. The vehicle is already packed. I have to share an overhanging strap with a young businessman who holds a newspaper in my face. The bus lurches and stops, but his balance is perfect; his eyes remain on the page.

Department stores and boutiques line the road. Here and there, vendors have spread their wares on the sidewalks. Women in spike heels pick their way past beggars.

I am so caught up in the pageantry of city life that I almost miss my stop. At the last minute, I manage to reach up and press the button signaling my need to get off. The bus jerks to the side of the road, opening its doors. I squeeze through a snarl of passengers and land on the sidewalk.

The Japanese Embassy is sparkly and clean. Two Indonesian guards stand at the gate, unsmiling. I state my business. One of them asks to see my passport and gives it a cursory examination.

"Just another English teacher," they are probably thinking.

Behind me, a trio of Indonesian women whip out passports of their own. I hear the word for "dancer" and shake my head. They'll end up in some dark bar, tangled up with gangsters. I've heard stories about locked-away documents, indentured slavery. I want to tell them to stay in Jakarta, but they are already through the gate.

Once inside, I find another crowd, but at least the place is air-conditioned. Even so, it's hot. I fill out the necessary forms, then pick up a brochure to fan myself with.

The lines move slowly. The Japanese men at the desk smoke

cigarettes and stamp papers. From time to time they scowl into the room. When they signed up for the Foreign Ministry, they were probably thinking Paris or Bonn. New York City.

When I finally make it to the desk, I stretch my lips into a smile. "*Onegai shimasu.*" I even bow.

Ten minutes later I have my visa.

• • • • •

While Philip is working, I wander around his apartment looking for clues. Why did he want me to come? Is this just a feel-good fling, something to ease his residual guilt? Or could he still be in love with me?

Right now I have nothing to go on. We've had great sex, dinners in expensive restaurants, and he's given me a bouquet of orchids. Romance, yes; I'm getting the Hollywood version. But settle-down-and-marry-me? He hasn't said that yet. So far we've talked about music, volcanoes, surfing, and the headhunters of Borneo. Except for that first night, we have not spoken of Kei or of the disastrous relationships that preceded this period. Maybe we are having "an affair to remember."

It has occurred to me that there is not enough room for Kei in this one-bedroom apartment. We'd have to move. He might not like that. Yet, he's always loved children, or said that he did. He told me that after his sister Nuala abandoned hers, he flew to Connecticut for a week to help Nick out. Good ol' Uncle Philip.

I go for a walk to clear my head. I'm accosted by beggars and durian sellers. I buy a satay at a stand and eat it under the awning.

"You English teacher?" the vendor asks.

I think for a moment. "Yes." I could reinvent myself here. Once again.

I have told Philip about hostessing. He was amused by my stories, but of course it is not the kind of career he respects. He has mentioned connections, secretarial jobs, but in an offhand way after several glasses of wine.

I lick my lips clean, toss my satay stick into a garbage can and thank the man. Then I wander some more. I go up and down the streets until my feet are blistered and I'm sure that I can sleep. When Philip comes home, I am taking a nap.

"Hey." He rolls me onto my back and kisses my mouth.

My arms twine around his neck, but he is all business.

"C'mon. Get up. We've got a plane to catch."

I squint into afternoon light and find the valise by the door. My board is leaning against it.

"Where are we going?" For a second, I wonder if he is sending me back to Japan.

"I'm taking you to the waves, baby. I got us a bungalow right on the beach."

"Oh, goodie."

I jump out of bed, smooth down my hair and toss the comforter over the rumpled sheets. A flash of fuchsia catches my eye. A sundress in a tropical print hangs from the closet door.

"Why don't you change? It'll help you get in the mood."

Five minutes later, we're zipping off to the airport, me in hibiscus, Philip in sunglasses and jeans. A vacation! To the beach!

I vaguely recall that other beach, the one in South Carolina where Philip's love for me unraveled. Oh, but this is supposed to be fun. Out, out dark thoughts.

Philip deals with the luggage and ushers me to a prop plane. The propellers are already spinning, blowing my hair and my dress. Up the clackety steps and we're in a cozy cave. A little ways away, I see a horde filing into a larger Air Garuda jet. But this craft—is it private?—makes me feel like a movie star. Suddenly, I'm special.

We can chat with the pilot in the cockpit, that's how snug it is. Philip asks questions in Indonesian. I am suitably impressed, but I don't understand a word. Then the pilot looks at me, runs his tongue over his top lip and winks at Philip.

Philip laughs a bit uncomfortably. He puts his arm around my shoulder. "Hey, she's my wife."

For a few moments, I am too shocked by his words to be frightened by our rock and roll ascent, too stunned to look out the window and take in the view. Sure, Philip was just trying to protect my virtue (my virtue!) but that word! On his lips!

Finally I am distracted by cabin service. A dark beauty who'd been sitting behind us till now comes forward with drinks on a tray. Blossoms adorn the glasses. I'm not sure what to do with mine—drink around it, or take it out? I remember that time Philip's sister served artichokes and I popped an entire butter-dipped leaf into my mouth, then chewed and chewed. My jaws kept grinding until I saw Philip skim the meat from the leaf with his teeth and then discard the rest.

Now, Philip plucks the pink flower from his glass and lays it on a napkin. I do the same. The taste is fruity, like a kiddie drink with a kick. Philip would know the name of it. I cast around for peanuts. There are none.

Out the window I can see islands everywhere. From here, they look like pelted rocks and sleeping whales. Philip points out one owned by a friend of his. That's not where we're going.

The plane begins its descent. The angle is so steep, it feels like we're diving. My drink sloshes in my stomach and threatens to erupt. At the last minute, Philip reattaches his seatbelt and a heartbeat later, we're bouncing along a makeshift runway.

Almost as soon as we land, we are whisked away to a Jeep and a driver in a white shirt. We blaze through palm trees, past rice fields and huts on stilts, to the far edge of the island.

Our bungalow is nestled among trees, but I can smell the ocean just beyond. I stand by as Philip tips the driver, then follow him inside. A ceiling fan stirs the air. Our feet glide across shiny teak floors. An orchid floats in a bowl of water on the table.

The windows are wide open. We can see white sand one way, a private pool another. We move like thieves, on to the bedroom, the king-sized bed enveloped in mosquito netting.

"Do you like it?" Philip stands by eagerly.

"Ooh. I love it." No lie. I whirl into his arms. Suddenly we're crashing onto the fantasy bed, tearing at tropical prints and denim, and rolling on starched white sheets.

It is heaven here, I think later, drinking coffee on the verandah. Philip feeds me banana bread from his fingertips. When the moon comes out, we slow dance by the pool and then we dive in, naked.

In the morning, Philip takes me to a reef. He carries my board and stakes out a spot on the sugar sand.

I have already warned him that I'm just a beginner. He assures me that this is a good beach for rookies. I see half a dozen fat Germans and their temporary native girlfriends, catch a few Australian accents on the light tropical breeze. At this hour, there are only a handful of surfers. Most of them are standing around in waist-deep water, waiting for a ride. They eschew the kind of waves that my Japanese surfing buddies would jump at. Maybe they made a mistake. Maybe they'd meant to go to Kuta Beach.

Philip lazes on the towel while I wax my board. My heart thumps like a rabbit. I want to ask him if there is a more deserted beach with no surfers and fewer spectators. And would he mind looking the other way when I am in the water?

But Philip cracks open a paperback spy novel and a beer, ignoring all of my preparations. He's seen surfing before, maybe even tried it himself.

My board all waxy and sticky, I flutter my fingers at him and trudge to the lip of the water. It's blood-warm around my ankles. I forge onward, looking for snakes.

I take on the swells that the others can't be bothered with, riding on my stomach to shore. And then, after about five runs, I try to get up on my knees. The first time, I tumble off my board and wind up sitting on a sand bar. I rein in my board and head back out. Philip may be watching, or not. I don't even look his way.

Finally, I see a wave approaching. It rolls toward me, gathering volume and might. It's not like the wimpy swells I've been riding till now. This one is a grown-up. A kahuna of waves.

My timing is perfect. I slap my body against the board and curl into a crouch. The wave lifts and carries me. Slowly, I unbend my body until at last, for one shining moment, I am a surfing goddess, standing on my board for the first time. The cerulean sky, the hiss of the ocean, the salt on my lips—all of it fuses into a flicker of transcendence. I've never heard of a surfer's high before, but this is it. My nirvana.

This time, wave breaking into froth at my feet, I descend from fiberglass with grace. I hear hoots and applause and look to shore. Philip's face is hidden by his book. The cheers are coming from the other surfers. I mock bow to them, as pleased as I am embarrassed. It's as if they know, somehow, that they'd witnessed my first real ride. My initiation is complete.

My first impulse is to hurl myself out of the water and call Eric. He'd be so proud of me. Why didn't I have Philip take a video? But then again, this is my own private victory. I will tell no one. I will treasure the memory and let the power of it build. It'll be something to sustain me in the days and weeks and months to come.

When I get back to Japan, I'm going to paint my board.

• • • • •

The night before I leave, we are in a French restaurant.

"So how about it?" Philip pours more wine into my glass. The candles cast strange shadows on his face, making him look like a ghoul.

"How about what?"

"Do you want to give it another try? Us? Together?"

I take a deep breath. "Yes. But there's one condition."

He freezes, the wine bottle still aloft. I'll bet he thinks I'm going to demand a band of gold.

"When I come back, I'm bringing Kei."

He sets the bottle down. "I thought you said you lost custody."

161

"I did, but only for a little while. Until I get back on my feet. Japanese divorce laws are kind of funny." I pinch myself under the table. Stop blathering.

"Well, I'd love to meet him." Philip eases back into his chair.

So now I'm thinking this man is my ticket out of Japan. Well, he owes it to me, doesn't he? After all, I never would have gone there had he not broken my heart. I would have gone to Cameroon. Maybe I'd be living there right now.

I can see myself sitting under a mango tree, watching elephants graze. Maybe I'm painting this scene, maybe not. I'm having thoughts about the terrain, the smiling children, the exotic smells of palm oil and baboon droppings, all in some other language. French, or Cameroonian.

I've never met Yusuke. I don't even know that he exists. He is probably on the other side of the globe, ensconced in his father's company as right-hand man, while his Japanese wife tends their brood and tries not to piss off Okaasan. It's none of my business.

Yusuke, who?

I'm having a wild, passionate affair with a man who looks exactly like Yannick Noah. He comes from the same Cameroonian village. He plays tennis, too, though not as well as his doppelganger. He's a conservationist or a professor or a doctor. He's educated and savvy in Western ways and though he loves his mother, he loves me more.

We don't have any kids. We'll have them in the future, maybe. Right now we hesitate to invite that kind of heartbreak into our lives. Children bring the most exquisite pain. We know this even without experience.

Kei does not exist. He's never been born.

No, wait. This is not the life that I want instead.

• • • • •

The next morning Philip drives me to the airport with enough leeway for souvenir shopping. He hovers behind me while I sift through batiked garments and strings of beads. The shops are filled with painted wooden animals and puppets, T-shirts, scarves. I fondle a rubber Komodo dragon, imagine Kei's delight at receiving it, and put it back down. I've already decided that I won't try to win him back with things. Besides, what if his grandmother found the toy and asked him where he'd gotten it? Could he lie? Would she know that the dragon was from Indonesia? Maybe they found out about my trip. Who knew what kind of tabs they were keeping on me? So nothing for Kei, not even a postcard. I pick out some batik scarves for my friends at the Cha Cha Club, and a tape of traditional Balinese music for Eric. He could play it during his yoga classes. And for Maya, I buy a T-shirt tie-dyed in sunset colors. It looks like something a deadhead would wear back home. I know it'll clash with her Chanel watch, but that's the point. I'm getting her what I think a high school girl should want.

As the cashier rings up my purchases, I become conscious of Philip once again. I wonder if he'll give me a Hollywood send-off. I imagine him dipping me for a kiss in the airport lobby or running alongside the plane shouting "I love you!"

He walks me to the gate and checks his watch.

"If you have to get to work or something, it's fine. You can leave. I'll be okay."

His eyes dart around. He rocks back on his heels. All that pent-up energy. Would I ever be able to hold him in place?

The boarding call comes across the loudspeaker. I don't get in line, not right away. I think about Sigourney Weaver in that movie, on the last plane out of Jakarta. How she sits there watching the runway for her man, wondering if he can step away from adventure for the love of her. Just when they're starting to fold up the walkway, when she'd given up all hope, he comes running toward the plane. Mel Gibson, with one eye patched, soaking with sweat. He runs toward her.

When everyone but me has filed onto the plane, Philip gives me a peck on the lips and says, "Alright, big girl. See you in a

163

couple months. Be good." He pats me on the bottom and I turn and walk away.

• • • • •

The next time I see Maya, she is wearing a diamond as big as the Keio Plaza. Ludicrous with her polyester school uniform.

"Wow," I say, as it nearly blinds me with a refracted ray. "Are you engaged or what?"

She blushes like a maiden. "It's from my boyfriend," she says, not really answering my question.

"He must be important."

"Yes. He is."

We take a moment to admire the facets in silence. We share the awe.

"Don't tell anyone, okay?" She leans forward, pleading. "Especially my mother."

I have to laugh. As if her mother would even speak to me. I nod. "Okay, I promise." I even lock pinkies with her to seal the vow, although it's not necessary; we are engaged in a kind of two-way blackmail.

On to the business at hand. "So what have you got for me this time?"

Maya grins. "My mother is babysitting Kei this week and I said I would help. I can bring him to the park to meet you."

All of the blood in my head rushes to my feet. I feel as if I am about to faint. It's almost too good to be true. I can't be this lucky.

"How did this come about?" My voice quakes. "What's Obaas-an doing?"

"She has to go to the hospital." Maya shrugs, as if it's something casual, but her eyes dart away from mine.

"The hospital?"

"She has digestion problems." Here, Maya gives her notes a glance. Then she blushes again. "My mother says she is worried about the wedding."

"The wedding?"

"Yes." Maya's voice is barely a whisper. "Mr. Yamashiro is getting married again. His fiancée is from an important family and this makes the grandmother nervous."

I'll bet.

• • • • •

A week later, I'm stepping into the Silver Bell Wedding Chapel in heels and a pastel polyester suit. The clothes are on loan from Betty. I don't have much in my closet these days besides surf-wear and sleazy hostess attire. Certainly nothing for a church wedding.

But this isn't really a church. It's a steepled playhouse on the roof of a hotel. The Caucasian clergyman in the choir robe isn't really a minister, either. He's probably an English teacher Monday through Friday, an actor-for-hire when a Western-style wedding comes up.

I slide into a pew at the front, next to Mama Morita. She's already got her hankie ready. I'm hoping her mascara is water-proof. I remember that Mama-san never took vows herself, and I wonder if at times like these she has regrets. Of course there is still time. You never know.

She reaches over and squeezes my hand. I pat hers back, scratching my palm on her rings.

A few more guests bustle into the chapel and then the "min-ister" nods to the organist, a Japanese woman in hot pink tulle, and Braham's wedding march fills our ears.

There are no little girls strewing rose petals, no parade of bridesmaids and ushers. Everyone turns to the entrance at the end of the aisle, but no one comes. Has she changed her mind? I look around the room, trying to read the faces of the others. It's then that I spot the tiny Filipina woman in glasses and bun, and the coffee-colored boy next to her. His hair still has comb tracks. He is wearing a powder blue suit. His face suddenly lights up and I turn to see that the doorway has filled with a cloud of white froth. The bride's two-hour make-up job is concealed by the veil. She moves slowly past the pews, in time with the music. She walks by herself. No one is giving this woman away. She has decided everything by herself.

As she approaches the altar, her waiting groom, the bursts of flowers, I see that the boy is leaning toward her. And Veronica, she's not looking at her husband-to-be. Even through the lace I can see that her gaze is directed at him. Her son. Luis. She winks at him and takes her place in front of Mr. Shima. He hesitates, then takes her hands, holds them as if they might break.

As the ceremony gets underway, I find myself diving into my purse for a tissue. Such plain hope on Shima-san's face! And Veronica's look of cool resignation. I pray that she will learn to love him. I wish them a thousand years of happiness—Veronica, Mr. Shima, and Luis.

# 1996

THE LAST TIME KEI AND I WERE TOGETHER, I TOOK HIM TO MCDON-
ald's, the one near the train station. He ate a cheeseburger (mi-
nus the pickles), an order of fries, plus half of mine, and a little
cup of vanilla ice cream. I can still see the smear of sticky white
on his upper lip.

"I've got tickets to a soccer game. Semi-professional," I said.
"Do you want to go?"

His smile blasted like a hundred suns. "When? When?" His
hand tugged on mine, as if he wanted to drag me off to the playing field right then.

"Next Saturday," I said. "We can take our lunch and eat it in
the stands." I was thinking about how I'd get up early and mold
rice balls in my hands, how I'd fill each one with a different surprise: pickled plums, bonito flakes sprinkled with soy sauce, tuna
and mayonnaise. There would be a thermos filled with hot chocolate and homemade cookies, both oatmeal and peanut butter,
and oranges in our pockets. We'd sit hip to hip on the bleachers,
buoyed by the excitement of the crowd. We'd float on cheers and
chants.

"What's your favorite pro team?" I asked.

"Bellmare," he said.

I nodded. Next chance, I'd watch them on TV.

"They've got Nakata. He's my hero."

I reached over and wiped the ice cream from his lip with my finger. "Well, you know what? You're my hero. I love you more than anything else in the world."

He squirmed, but he was smiling. "I love you too, Mom. So why can't I live with you?"

The rumble of a train pulling into the station resonated on my bones. What if we just hopped aboard one of those cars and let it carry us as far as it would go? Maybe we'd end up in the mountains where the ancient emperor's family hid out. We could set up a home in the brambles and chop down the vine bridge that swung over the gorge. We'd feast on berries and wild boar and no one would ever find us.

"You know what? I want you to live with me, but Obaasan and Daddy want you to live with them. It's two against one." I'd meant to speak lightly, but his eyes darkened. His eyebrows scrunched together.

"I'm going to get you back," I said. "I'll find a way for us to be together. I promise you."

My heart was hammering. What if he went back and told his grandmother what I'd said? For an instant, I thought about extracting a vow of silence. But I didn't.

"Anyway, you've got soccer practice, right?"

His features softened. He nodded.

"So let's get you back home. And then you can start ticking off the days till the big game next week-end."

• • • • •

On the following Saturday, I showed up at the appointed time and rang the doorbell. Not even door-to-door salesmen bothered with the bell. Most visitors just went ahead and slid the door open and called out a greeting, since the entryway was considered public space. But I, who'd once lived in this house, could not bring myself to do that.

I could hear the singsong chime on the other side of the door, then footsteps. Not the sound of my son's puppy-dog scramble, but the measured, muted steps of Yusuke's mother.

She slid open the door and raised her eyebrows. "*Hai?*"

"I've come to pick up Kei for the soccer game. I promised him—"

"Oh, well, I'm sorry. He's not here now. He went to Awajishima for the day with a friend."

Awaji Island? To the amusement park? To the zoo with koalas? I'd taken him there just two weeks before.

"But we had plans. I told you. I told Yusuke."

She shrugged. Her hand was on the door, eager to pull it shut. "I guess Kei changed his mind."

"I don't believe you. He was so excited when I told him."

"Maybe he was just pretending to make you happy."

I had never hated her as much as I did at that moment. I suddenly knew that she had been plotting against me. If Kei had truly chosen not to go to the game, then it was because she'd threatened him or lied to him. Maybe she'd even told him that I'd canceled our plans.

"What time will he be back?" I had half a mind to sit there on the porch till he came home. Then I could explain everything to him, and I would be able to see in his eyes what he truly felt.

"It's hard to say," she said. "I'll tell him that you were here."

# 1997

SO FINALLY HE IS THERE BEFORE ME. HIS FACE IS SMUDGED WITH dirt and chocolate, his hair in disarray. He has learned how to shield his soul and I can not see into his eyes. More than anything I want to pull him into my arms, but he stands so stiffly. He needs time to melt.

"I've missed you," I say. I'm half-afraid he's forgotten English and I can't bring myself to speak in the grandmother tongue.

"You've grown." Banal, but true. His heft is alien to me. Those extra kilograms cause a spasm of grief.

He has taken a vow of silence. His lips are pressed firmly together, but he keeps his eyes on me. What have they told him? What lies? What kind of curse is holding him back?

"You know, Kei, I didn't want to leave you. You're the most precious thing in the world to me." Still, nothing, and my voice is starting to crack. "I love you. You must know that."

I refrain from prostration. At his age, it might seem frightening. I must maintain control. I have to show him that I am strong and capable of protecting him.

"Kei," I say. "I'm going to have to leave Japan. Your father and grandmother don't want me here, and I feel so very sad. So I'm leaving. But I want you to come with me. If you want to, that is. You don't have to stay with me forever, but we could spend some time together. Go to soccer games. Disneyland."

He looks down and kicks at the dirt.

"Kei, do you understand what I said?

A little nod then, and I see a tear drop onto his shoe.

"Do you know how to use the telephone?"

Another nod.

I hand him an envelope. He takes it without looking at me.

"This is my telephone number. You can call me any time, okay? But try to do it secretly, when your grandmother is sleeping or something. She might get angry, but you do have the right to call me. I'm your mommy."

I wish he would say something, anything, even if it's cruel. I reach out to touch his hair, afraid that he will dissolve like a ghost. He remains, tense and still.

The strands are still baby soft. I close my eyes to better concentrate on this instant. I can smell his little boy sweat, juice on his breath. His heat. And then I force my hand back to my side, knowing better than to ask for a hug.

"I'll come here tomorrow," I say. "If you want to see me then, I'll be here."

• • • • •

The next afternoon, I arrive early and stake out a spot. My high nose, my aloneness, draw stares and furtive peeks. A young mother in platform shoes pushes a baby carriage past me. Even though she, with her dyed-orange hair and multiply pierced ears is arguably more of a spectacle than I am, she stumbles when she sees me.

I feel like following her, shouting out advice. Right now that tiny baby, so engrossed with his star-shaped hands, doesn't yet know how to break his mother's heart. But he'll learn the power of a shrug, a sigh, an averted gaze. He'll memorize all the words that can puncture and scar. Someone will teach him. His grandmother. His father. The kids at the playground.

A soccer game takes shape on the field. I can't make out the division of teams. They all seem to be kicking the ball every which way. They're boys, about seven or eight, a little older than Kei. One kid kicks the ball into an arc so high it looks like it'll eclipse the sun.

I am enjoying this—the game, the laughter, the wind on my face. The hills brushed with goldenrod, the plush grass beneath my feet. I pretend that it's enough.

He doesn't come. I wait until the mothers and their babies have gone home for supper, till the future soccer stars scatter and disappear. The moon brightens, the sky deepens to indigo.

My watch tells me that I'm going to be late for work. I drag myself back to the bus stop with a clear vision in my head—yesterday, Kei, within three feet.

Anything could have happened. His grandmother might have taken him shopping. He might have been trapped by some TV show. Kids get involved in their imaginary worlds. They forget things. Or maybe he'd wanted to come, but he'd been scared to venture out on his own. Maybe in that household there are rules about that sort of thing.

I don't have to wait long for a bus. Luckily there's an empty seat near the back. I slide over to the window and watch the tile-roofed houses flashing by.

I replay yesterday's meeting over and over, trying to summon scents and the taste of the air. In my mind I see the shadow of Kei's lashes on his cheek, moons of dirt beneath his fingernails. That loose button, hanging by a thread. The top of his head, burnished by rays.

When I get off the bus, I rush back to my apartment and check for phone messages. Nothing from Kei. Not even a hang-up. Just a message from Eric confirming tomorrow morning's surfing lesson.

I change into a red polyester dress and fishnet tights and hot-foot it to the club. When I walk in, all eyes go to the clock. I'm two hours late.

Not that it matters. It's not like we're punching a time clock here and none of us are on salary. I'm not going to be punished, but I know that I have provoked curiosity. I'm almost always on time.

I slide onto a stool at the bar to catch my breath and wait for directives. Mama Morita is behind the bar, filling a bowl with mixed nuts.

"Why don't you join Betty and her group?" She indicates the table where our hostess is single-handedly entertaining five men at once.

Betty's not gorgeous like Veronica. She's a bit plump and heavy-handed with the blue eye shadow, but she's always in demand as a raconteur. Right now she is mid-story, fully animated, and all of her clients are writhing with laughter.

Mama Morita offers me a glass of club soda. I take a few sips and then pull up a seat across from Betty. The men hardly notice me, so I'm allowed to lapse into deep thought.

Why didn't Kei show up? Is it because he's just six and not brave enough to venture across the road on his own? Not allowed by his grandmother? Or was I too intense yesterday? Maybe I made him uncomfortable with my declarations of undying love. After all, who knows what kind of lies his grandmother and father have been spinning about me? What if I give him some kind of incentive to come and see me? What would he want?

"Betty-chan," the man next to me blurts out. "Tell that story about the priest and the monkey again. The one you told last week."

The other men, remembering, start laughing before she has even begun.

"Yes, tell it," another guy says.

And I get an idea.

• • • • •

"Maya? Hi, it's me. Do you think you could bring Kei to the riverside park again today?"

There is a long silence on the other end of the phone. I'm wondering if she's still there, when she says, "I'm a little bit busy today."

173

"Maya, I'll give you a bonus. Please. I really need to see him." I'm broke and I can't afford a bribe like this, but I am desperate.

"What should I say? My mother isn't babysitter today."

"I don't know. Say you had fun the other day and you want to play with Kei. Say you're thinking about becoming a kindergarten teacher in the future."

I can almost see her chewing on her pink-frosted lip. Finally, after about a minute, she sighs. "Okay. Four o'clock."

When Maya escorts Kei to the park, I lead him to a bench in the shade of an oak tree. Maya lingers for a moment until I hand her an envelope and shoo her away. Watching her retreat, the heels of her thigh-high vinyl boots and kinked streaky hair, I wonder why the Yamashiros are so quick to trust her with my son.

It could be they are distracted by wedding plans. Or perhaps the image of the younger Maya, innocent, black-haired and soft spoken, is so deeply etched that they can not quite see what she has become.

Across the field she pauses and checks her pager. Maybe she's got a message from Mystery Man. For all I know, she will use this opportunity to arrange a quick meeting with him. Which is fine by me, as long as she keeps Kei out of it.

"So how are you today?" I ask him. I want to kiss him, but I don't dare.

He stares at his knees.

"*Genki?*"

"*Genki,*" he confirms, looking up at me through his lashes.

"Good. Well, guess what? I brought a book to read to you today. Do you remember when I used to read books to you?"

He nods.

"Do you remember '*Goodnight Moon*'?"

He nods again.

"Babar? Madeline? The little dog named Spot?"

He doesn't answer but I catch him studying the red-covered volume in my hands: *My Father's Dragon*. I tell him that it was my favorite book growing up, that it's an adventure story about a little boy named Elmer Elevator who runs away from home to save a baby dragon.

"Does it sound interesting? Shall I read?"

He just looks up at me through his lashes.

"Okay." I clear my throat and open the book. "Chapter One. My Father Meets the Cat."

• • • • •

The next day I buy a soccer ball. I hold it on my lap as the bus takes me to Tokushima. It's smooth and cool under my hands. The smell of new vinyl rises up to me. It's a virgin ball. I thought about kicking it, about having Eric teach me some tricks, but then I changed my mind. This'll be something we share from the start.

When the bus gets to my stop, I jostle down the aisle, ball held in front of me, shielding my tender heart. I go down the step and down the hill toward the park, think about going across the road and catching the bus in the other direction. What if he isn't there? I stop in my tracks, close my eyes, suck in a deep breath. When I open my eyes, he is there. Alone. A miracle.

I run down the hill. My boy is crouching in the grass, his T-shirt hiked up, revealing a strip of pale skin. His clothes are too small. Don't they notice, his grandmother and Yusuke? Or are they so caught up in this wedding business that they can't be bothered?

A T-shirt, I think. I will buy him a new T-shirt. Even though he can't wear it. They would notice that, wouldn't they? They would ask him where it came from.

I am a few feet away when he looks up. I see a flash of joy, but then it is gone, concealed by that wary mask.

I hold the ball out to him. "Maybe you can teach me a few things. Can you show me how to dribble?"

He comes closer, like a squirrel accepting a nut. He whisks the ball away from me, throws it high into the air. As it comes down, he positions himself under it and then sends it up again with his knee.

I clap in surprise. "That's wonderful!"

His smile is huge. Somehow, I understand that no one has praised him like that. Not since I left. "What else can you do?" I ask.

He doesn't say a word, but stops the ball with his foot and starts dribbling it down the field. After awhile, he pivots, moves back, and runs in to the ball, sending it flying with a well-placed kick. Flying to me.

• • • • •

He comes the next afternoon, and the one following that. By now, we are on chapter three.

"What did Elmer Elevator pack in his knapsack?" I ask. "Do you remember?"

"Mmm." Kei touches his lower lip. "Chewing gum?"

"Yes! What else?"

"Pink lollipops, rubber bands, toothpaste, six magnifying glasses…"

"Very good. Anything else?"

"Peanut butter sandwiches."

"Yes! Twenty-five peanut butter sandwiches. Isn't that something?"

That he has been listening, that he has understood, that he is as interested as six-year-old-me—all this is enough to bring tears to my eyes. Outright sobbing would probably alarm him, though, so I crack open the book and start on the next chapter.

An occasional gust of wind rustles the pages. Dead leaves dance at our feet. Kei leans against my arm, peering over at the illustrations.

He likes the picture of the gum-chewing tigers and the one of Elmer Elevator on the tip of a rhino's horn.

We get to the part about the rhino's weeping pool. Here, I pause and close the book on my thumb. "What," I ask, "do you think the rhino is crying about?"

Kei looks across the field at the boys playing soccer, and then up at the sky. "*Okaasan ga inai kara.*" Because he doesn't have a mother.

I draw him close without thinking and bury my face in his neck. "Oh, no," I say. "It's nothing so tragic as that." I feel his body grow soft. When I loosen my arm, he looks up at me and his eyes are full of want. He is asking for more than just a story.

Before I can help myself, the words are out of my mouth: "How would you like to run away with me and find a real dragon?"

• • • • •

She is beautiful, my mermaid, if I do say so myself. I've painted her scales with an iridescent green so that she'll shimmer and flash on the waves. Her hair is the color of coral, the tresses of a Tintoretto, all curly and flaming. Cockle shells are strung around her neck. Her arms are folded over her breasts. She's almost too pretty to stand on. I am tempted to hang her on the wall. But I don't. As soon as the paint is dry and sealed under urethane, I give her a name—Esmerelda—and take her out for a test run.

I'm a little embarrassed when I first step onto the sand. I remind myself of those Japanese skiers who, having spent a wad on parkas and top-of-the-line gear, look like a million yen going up in the chairlift but fall down as soon as their skis hit the snow. I feel like a fashion surfer. But no one cares.

As soon as I've unzipped my case, Esmerelda draws squeals of delight. A flock of young women in waterproof make-up and wetsuits scuttle over for a look.

"*Kawaii! Doko de katta no?*"

I tell them that I bought this board at a second-hand shop, that it's the same one they've seen me struggling on all these weeks.

"I painted it myself."

"*Honto?*" More squeals, and then they are tugging at my arm, spewing their visions. One girl wants a manga character—Sailor Moon—painted on her board. Another, a scene of Hawaii.

"How much?" one girl asks.

I throw out what I believe to be an astronomical figure. They exchange glances, murmur and giggle. "*Yasui, ne?*"

Cheap, they say. Well, they're all working part-time and living with their parents. I suppose I should have asked for more money. I've seen their Gucci cell-phone holders.

Before I've even had a chance to test Esmerelda's seaworthiness, before my surfing master arrives at the scene, I've garnered five commissions: Enough to get me out of debt. I ought to have some left over for a present for Kei. A Gameboy. A robot. Whatever he wants.

I'm taking down phone numbers and addresses when I hear a loud "Harumph."

"Good morning, Eric."

The young women greet him in chorus. I see one of them jab another, and I know they've got crushes. I wonder just how long Eric will hold out.

For now, he's above it all, his mind already on the sea.

"Okay. Jill. Have you stretched? Are you ready to get wet?" Then he sees Esmerelda. "Hey, I think I'm in love."

"I could paint your board, too," I say. "After all, I owe you big time."

"I'll keep that in mind."

• • • • •

I'm leaving. I have already packed my bag. I've sorted through my possessions and shipped the most essential to my mother. The rest is destined for flea markets or trash or friends. I wrap up my crystal wine glasses and pottery cups in newspaper and pay a visit to Veronica.

When she opens the door, I catch a whiff of varnish and wood. Her hair is bundled in a bandanna. The sleeves of her gingham shirt are rolled up, the hem hanging out over her faded blue jeans. Most importantly, she's gained a couple of pounds and her cheeks are rosy.

"Long time no see," I say. I hand over the dishes and give her a hug.

"What's this?" she asks.

"Oh, I was just cleaning. I thought you might need those more than I do."

She frowns in confusion. "Well, thanks. Come in, come in. I made cookies. Let's have some coffee."

Indeed, a gust of cinnamon greets me as I step into the foyer. I follow Veronica into the kitchen where jet and ship-shaped cookies cool on a rack.

"For Luis," she says, "but my husband likes them, too."

The huge windows and white walls fill the room with light. Such a contrast to that dark den where we spent so many nights. I feel a twinge of regret. In spite of everything, I will miss the Cha Cha Club—Betty, Mama Morita, Yuko, even some of the clients.

While the coffee is brewing, Veronica pulls a photo album from the bookshelf. "We went to Huis Ten Bosch," she says, opening to the first page. And there they are, in the artificial Dutch village, Luis, Veronica, and Shima-san smiling, against a backdrop of tulips. The next picture features the same setting, but Veronica's mother has taken Shima-san's place. Later, all four of them pose in front of a windmill.

"How is Luis?" I ask. "Does he like it here?" A glance at the clock tells me he'll be home from school soon.

Veronica's eyes get that faraway look that I remember from our dinners, but she quickly reels herself back into the room. "He misses his friends. It will take some time for him to adjust. But yes, I think he likes it here."

Next month, Shima-san is taking them to Disneyland, she tells me.

"I guess he won't be coming back to the Cha Cha Club," I say. I mean it as a joke, but Veronica's face is serious.

"Oh, no. He comes home every evening straight from work. We eat dinner together, the four of us."

Watching her, I try to believe that my happiness is possible, too. I imagine eating dinner with Kei every evening, baking cookies for him. Once again, I'm tempted to tell her of my plan, but the fewer people who know about it, the better. In my nightmares, the henchman twists arms and necks, wrenching information from the people I love.

• • • • •

It is morning. I'm hiding behind a tree, my heart banging. A mosquito alights on my arm, but I don't dare brush it away, can't move, can't draw attention to myself. I'm wearing dark glasses and a scarf over my pre-Raphaelite curls, barely breathing.

A woman walks by and doesn't give me and my tall nose even a glance. The camouflage seems to be working.

Children are filing into the schoolyard. Canteens bounce against their thighs, bags swing as they stride. My eyes dart from boy to boy. I wait and wait, each second an hour, a day, a week. Finally, I see a familiar gait, the glint of red in his hair. The sunburnished cheeks. He's shading his eyes from the glare and I think that he sees me. I step out of the shadows and wave.

He lurches a little toward me, then catches himself. I watch as he moves at the center of a group, the core protected.

He draws nearer. His eyes are on mine. I smile. I beckon.

His gaze flicks away to the sidewalk, to the boys surrounding him. He stops in his tracks, bends down to adjust his shoe. The other boys leave him behind. He is alone, exposed and I reach out my hand.

He comes to me, curious.

Maya has already called the school to say that he won't be attending today. A slight cold. It will be hours before he is missed.

"Hi." I draw him into the shadows, down a side street. "Are you ready for our adventure?"

He shrugs, then nods.

I bend down and hold his shoulders. "We're going to the airport and then we're going to fly on an airplane. We'll go see a dragon."

180

"*Obaachan wa?*"

I nod, trying to stay calm. My palms are starting to perspire. "We'll call Obaachan when we get there. We'll send her a post card."

"Otousan?"

"We'll send him a postcard, too."

He cocks his head to one side as if he's not quite sure he believes me.

I jiggle his shoulders a little. "It'll be fun. And if you don't like it, I'll bring you straight back here."

I hear a gate open behind us and all of my muscles tighten. I turn to see an elderly woman set out a saucer of milk.

"Come on." I jerk him forward a little.

He looks up, surprised by my roughness.

"Sorry," I say. "But we have to hurry. We've got a ferry to catch."

On the ferry, Kei keeps watch for dolphins. He leans against the railing, salty wind whipping his hair, while I hang on to the tail of his shirt. Of course he will not fall overboard. He won't jump. It's just an excuse to almost touch him.

"When we get to Indonesia, I'll show you a Komodo dragon!" I've already promised this, but I want to remind him. This isn't going to be like eating cereal in a hotel room. We're embarking on a grand adventure. And I'm different now. I haven't had a cigarette in over a month. I've stopped drinking, more or less. I can stand on a surfboard and ride a wave. I can take care of him now.

"*Achi!*" he says, excited.

I'm a little sad that he is speaking Japanese. It's as if all of the English words I taught him have been scrubbed out of his head. In other words, he's still brainwashed.

"I think it's just a buoy," I say, hating myself a little.

He slumps in disappointment, turns away from the rail. "*Hara heta.*" I'm hungry.

"Well, then. I'll buy you something to eat."

He ignores my bright smile and stumbles past me, into the passenger compartment. I steer him toward the snack bar on the second level. He wants chips and ice cream. A rice ball wrapped in dried seaweed. A box of chocolates. I lay down a crisp bill and buy it all for him. He snatches the chips out of my hand and tears the bag open with his teeth.

"Hey. How about a 'thank you'?"

Sheepishly, because he's been schooled in manners after all, he does a little head bow and says, "San kyu." Purely Japanese pronunciation.

I try not to be annoyed.

This is what I want to say: "Quit acting as if you are doing me some huge favor. I am your mother and if you grow up without me, there will be a hole in your life forever. Later on, you'll be happy. Trust me." But even if I did say it, he probably wouldn't understand it in English.

"*Oishii?*" I ask, watching him lick the paper wrapping of his ice cream bar. "Does it taste good?"

He nods and then—this almost brings tears to my eyes—offers it up to me.

I take a bite.

This is the moment where I start to believe that everything will turn out fine.

I let the ice cream melt on my tongue and keep it in my mouth for as long as I can without swallowing.

He takes a few more bites and then he holds it out to me again.

For the rest of the ride, we sit there eating snacks.

"Do you remember how you used to like Spaghetti-Os?" I ask him.

He cocks his head.

"You know, those little round noodles in tomato sauce?"

I can tell that he's doing his best, but there's no flash of recognition.

"Oh, well. When we get to America you might remember."

Right now what I really want to do is cook him a meal—something wholesome like vegetables cut into hearts and stars and then steamed to crispness; chicken dipped in egg and crushed cornflakes and then oven fried; macaroni and cheese made from scratch. The kind of stuff my own mom made for me. But that'll come later.

As we pull into port, Kei allows me to draw him into a hug. I feel him soften against me.

He carries his little rucksack, the one he lugged to kindergarten every day, and I strap the other bags over my shoulders. They're heavy. I'm wobbling like an aged packhorse as we cross the gangway.

A bus is already waiting to take us to the airport terminal, which is within sight. I resist the urge to dash for it and try to match my steps with Kei's. He is serious and quiet as he sits beside me. The jets grab his attention.

"You rode an airplane before," I tell him. "When you were three. Do you remember?"

He shakes his head and then shrugs. "A little. We watched a movie and drank chocolate milk."

"That was fun, right? This'll be fun, too. We're going to have a great trip."

"Otousan took me to Disneyland last summer," he says.

I wonder if he's already missing his father, if their bond was that great.

"There's a Disneyland in America, too. Disney World."

He looks at me with interest. "Do they have dragons there?"

"I don't think so, Kei. The Komodo dragons are on an island. I don't think you can see them anywhere else."

"Not even in the zoo?"

"Well, maybe."

The bus screeches to a halt and we head for the check-in counter.

"Passports, please," says the woman in the Air Garuda uniform.

I fumble in my purse, then lift out two navy blue booklets. "This is my son's," I say, pointing to the one on top.

Her fingers gallop across the keyboard. Her eyes graze the photos and then we've got bulkhead seats, no smoking, no problem. Our luggage is hoisted onto the conveyor belt and floats away. Suddenly I'm feeling lighter in spirit as well as body. I hang on tight to our tickets with one and glue the palm of my other to Kei's.

We've got time to kill, but I feel exposed in the lobby. I want to get Kei past all the checkpoints, to some place of almost no return.

"Let's go see what they've got in Duty Free Shopping," I say. "Maybe we'll find some candy."

Kei is dazed by the masses—lots of Japanese tourist families pushing brand-new hard-sided suitcases, and the groups that swarm around the flag-wielding guides. But there are also women with veils and saris, men with skin as dark as nougats, and pale-faced, fair-haired visitors from the far north. We hear bits of French, Arabic and Chinese. An American man calls to his spouse, "Honey, come here and have a look at this!" His voice is so loud, he's so tall and pasty; I wonder if I am just as obvious.

I tug Kei past these wonders to the security checkpoint. A guy ahead of us is wearing a turban—a Sikh, probably, on his way to India. He seems calm and composed even when the baby-faced guard at the conveyor belt asks him to step aside and starts rifling through his carry-on.

The next passengers, a Japanese family, make it through without any fuss.

I unhitch Kei's rucksack from his shoulders and lay it on the conveyor belt. Then, my own bag goes down. I watch the monitor, see my book, my extra T-shirt, a bag of dried mangoes X-rayed in black and white. We saunter through the metal detector. I reach for my bag.

"Step over here, please." The guard motions us over to the table off to the side. They're just picking on the foreigners, I think, as a heavily made-up Japanese woman glides past. I sigh. It'll be good to get away.

"Shall we go and get some juice?" I ask Kei. I'm trying to ignore this guy pawing through my tampons.

He nods. "There's the Pokemon plane," he says, pointing to the window, "Are we going to ride on that?"

"Maybe next time. If you really want to."

He looks up at me and grins. My half-hearted promise is almost a lie, but for that smile, I will try to make it happen. I will, I will.

But then, the guard dumps the contents of Kei's bag onto the table. I hadn't thought to look inside up till now, and I'm curious about what he's been carrying. There's a comic book, a change of clothes, a pack of cards. There's also a brocade charm, the kind sold at temples for safety on a journey or success at passing a college entrance examination. The guard picks this up and turns it over in his hand. Something falls out of it. He brings it to his nose, then he rips it open. Dried leaves spill into his palm. At first I think it's tea, but then I realize that it's not and I feel my bowels freeze.

The guard looks at me. His eyes are cold. "Your passports, please," he says. Then he speaks into his walkie talkie.

I reach for Kei's hand.

My palm is starting to sweat. My hairline, the small of my back, under my arms. Japanese tourists surge past us, on to their vacations in Hawaii or Sydney or Guam. We stand rooted for what seems like hours, but the minute hand on my watch moves slowly. Then Kei says, "Look. A policeman."

Actually, there are several. They move toward us with the force of wind. People lean away from them as if blasted by their presence. In my own country, there would be a hum. Here, there is sudden and complete silence.

"Yamashiro Jill-san?" the youngest one asks. "We want to ask you a few questions." His English is perfect. He must have studied abroad.

"What about my son?" I ask, drawing Kei close to me.

This doesn't merit a response. I notice then that one of them is wearing a skirt. She holds out a hand to Kei and, knowing this could get ugly, I nudge him forward.

"Mommy." He grabs at my sleeve. His eyes are huge.

"You'll be okay sweetie," I whisper. "They just want to talk a little. I'll come back to you as soon as I can." I'm lying, I know. I try to smile for Kei, but my eyes fill with tears and then I don't care what he or anyone else thinks. I get down on my knees and gather him against me. His arms go around my neck, and I can feel his body trembling, can feel his wet breath at my ear. He is crying.

"Yamashiro-san." Someone touches my shoulder.

The hand is gentle, but I can imagine them trying to pry us apart, and that would be more than I can bear. So I let him go. "I love you, Kei," I say, looking straight into his eyes. "Don't ever forget that."

"Mommy, I love you, too."

I am losing my son again.

They take me away from him, to a toilet where I am asked to pee in a cup, and then to a room with a table and two folding chairs. I sit there, with my head in my hands. What is happening to my son? Did the police officers find the phone number and Tokushima address written on the flap of his rucksack? Did they call his father or is he in the custody of strangers?

The light overhead is too bright. A little camera peers down from the corner of the ceiling. A cop comes in and sits down across from me at the table.

"Why are you trying to smuggle marijuana?" he asks.

"I'm not," I say. "I don't smoke marijuana. I have never smoked it."

I try to remember what I've heard about Paul McCartney. He tried to enter Japan with half a kilo of marijuana, which he told officials was for his personal use. Although he spent a few days in jail, he was ultimately deported. Fans objected to his arrest.

Officials said that since he was ignorant of the laws of this country, they'd let him go.

"I'm very sorry," I say. "I wasn't trying to smuggle drugs. I didn't know that my son was carrying marijuana. I didn't pack his bag. Someone must have planted it. I should have been more careful. I'm very, very sorry."

"Who packed the bag?"

I could say her name, but I don't. Misguided though she may be, underneath it all, Maya is still a kid. She's sweet at the core. I don't want to ruin her life, not when she still has a chance to straighten out.

"His grandmother. Setsuko Yamashiro." What the hell. It's not as if they'll arrest her. "We took the ferry here. I think my son may have put his bag down for a moment to go to the bathroom. Maybe someone put it in his bag on the boat. I really have no idea. It wasn't me. Please believe me."

I remember something else. I've heard that Japanese officials tend to be more lenient with those who are repentant. It's important to grovel.

"I'm very, very sorry, Officer, for the trouble I have caused you. I should have been more vigilant about our belongings. I feel sick that my son was carrying something illegal. I love him more than anything in the world. I beg your forgiveness." I look down at the floor, choking back tears.

He sighs. "You will have to stay with us for awhile."

I am escorted out of the lobby, out of the airport, to a police car at the curb. An hour later, I am sitting in a dingy cell with a couple of teen-aged prostitutes, staring at a stain on the wall. The girls whisper to each other about me. I am too tired to care.

I think about Maya, tucking a charm into Kei's bag; Philip, standing at the arrivals gate in Jakarta; the gangster who hassled me at the Cha Cha Club; Maya riding in Yusuke's car; the last sight I had of my son's face. When will I get to make a phone call? Will Gotonda-san be able to help me this time?

The futon provided for me is thin and worn. I'm exhausted,

but I can't sleep. All through the night, I think about Kei. In the morning, the guard brings bowls of *wakame* soup. I slurp under the gaze of my cellmates.

"Next is exercise time," one of them says to me. "And also cigarette smoking time."

"Exercise," I repeat. I wonder if we'll be doing *rajio taiso,* those choreographed movements that start out every sports festival in Japan.

But when breakfast is over and our bowls are cleared away, two guards come. The cell is unlocked and the other girls are led in one direction, me in another. I am taken to a room and abandoned. I stand there for a few minutes, wondering if I should start doing jumping jacks or something. Then, behind me, the door opens again. I turn to see Yusuke. Somehow I am not surprised. I am by now fairly certain that he and his goons have something to do with my detainment.

He looks tired. Disappointed. And also, somehow, relieved. His suit is neatly pressed, his cheeks shaven clean.

"Sit down," he says softly.

I look him in the eye. "I'm sorry." And I am. I'm sorry that I got caught, that I didn't get custody of my son, that I let him walk out of that hotel room with Yusuke, that I couldn't take Kei to that soccer game. At times, I am sorry that I came to this country in the first place, sorry that I went to that gallery opening and agreed to have a cup of coffee with the man I later married, sorry that I married him, sorry that I couldn't be happy living with his mother. There's more, but mostly I'm sorry in general.

Yusuke has always liked apologies. He nods and gestures once again to the chair.

This being Japan, I half expect someone to bring in a couple cups of green tea on a tray. It would be a nice distraction. But no one comes.

"How is Kei?" I ask after Yusuke seats himself.

"He's alright. He's with my mother."

I nod. "What did you tell him?"

"I made up a story about your passport."

"Oh. Good. Thank you." Thank you for not saying that his mother is a drug smuggler and a kidnapper.

Yusuke takes a pack of cigarettes out of his pocket and offers me one.

"No, thank you. I quit. But you go ahead."

I watch as he stabs a cigarette into his mouth and lights the tip. Breathes in, breathes out.

"Try to imagine," I say, "Growing up without a mother."

He takes another drag.

It occurs to me that I've miscalculated. Although he's never said so, perhaps he has imagined himself freed from his filial obligations, free from his mother's expectations. Maybe he, too, has had fantasies of us living in another country, happy, in love, with our family.

I take a deep breath. "Try to imagine that your mother loves you and wants to see you, but your father won't permit it. Or your father lies and says that your mother doesn't love you, doesn't care about you. What would it be like to grow up like that?"

He sighs and stubs out his barely smoked cigarette.

"If you wanted to punish me, you've succeeded. But it's not fair to punish Kei."

He shifts in his chair a little. "I understand how you feel."

"Do you?"

"Yes, but my mother, she is very angry."

My skin goes all clammy. For a minute there, I felt as if I were getting through.

Yusuke reaches into his jacket pocket once more and pulls out a thick envelope. "Take this," he says, "and get out of here. I've done what I could. You won't be charged, but you have to leave the country. Go back to America. Start a new life. You can talk to Kei later, but for now, you must leave . You've caused enough trouble already."

"*You can talk to Kei.*" Those words are like shining jewels. I

189

hold them in my mind, careful not to crush them, and I take the money.

Yusuke stands up to go. "By the way, I'm getting married next weekend. I thought you should know."

"Congratulations," I say. "But remember. That woman will never love Kei as much as I do."

He stands and tugs on his lapels. "Well. Good luck."

• • • • •

On the eve of my deportation, I'm sitting in a cold cell, neon flashing through the window. I'm booked on a flight to South Carolina and at the moment it doesn't seem so bad. Even Blondelle Malone eventually went back to Columbia. After her visit to Japan and her voyage to Europe, after hanging out with Mary Cassatt and Monet in France, her father called her back. And she went.

For a few minutes, I thought about trying to get to Africa, but I realized that I didn't need to go there anymore. I'd wanted to go someplace where small things took on importance, where a glass of clean water could make me believe in God. In Africa, I'd imagined that every day was intense: the heat, the hunger, the very struggle to stay alive. I was born into a middle-class family in a prosperous, peaceful country. There was no obvious war to protest, no important cause that caught my attention. But I had wanted to suffer. I was so young then. Look what happened to me. I no longer had to borrow misery. I'd created it all by myself.

# Epilogue

Jill Yamashiro
Dragon House Surfboard Designs
1046 Oceanview Drive
Myrtle Beach, South Carolina 29---
U.S.A.
September 4, 1998

Dear Jill-san,

I think you must be very angry with me. I am writing to say I'm sorry for the trouble I make. My boyfriend gave me charm. I didn't know its contents. I think happy journey for Kei. That is all.

I got sick of my boyfriend. He was a yakuza guy, no good manners. I have new boyfriend now, soccer player at school. Very handsome boy. I send you picture next time.

Anyway, I think you be interested to know that Yamashiro grandmother pass away last week. She have cancer, but it was secret. The funeral was very big. Many peoples come.

I hope you very happy in new life in America. I visit you sometime, okay?

Well, bye bye.

Love,

Maya

A few months after Yusuke's mother's death, we started to patch things up. I called long-distance from Myrtle Beach to Tokushima, and Yusuke put Kei on the phone.

"Hi. It's Mommy." I was afraid that he'd forgotten all of his English, even if he remembered me.

"Where are you?" This, a little surly, as if I was late picking him up from soccer practice, not in exile from his life.

"I'm in your other country," I said. "I've got a room all made up for you, but you can change it if you like. Paint the walls black, for all I care. Kei, are you listening?"

"Well, when can I come and visit?"

Now, I want to say. I'll be on the next plane to pick you up. But we've suffered from my impulses before.

"I'll have to talk to your dad about that, but I'll be ready for you whenever you get here."

After that, I started calling once a week. I wrote letters, too, and sent gifts that I could barely afford. And as soon as I managed to convince Yusuke to hook up to the Internet, I started sending e-mail and he wrote back.

"I miss you, Mommy," he wrote. "I love you."

He didn't write about his father's new wife, and I didn't ask. Yusuke told me himself when she became pregnant.

"Look, I need to see my son," I told him. "If you won't let him live with me, at least let me visit him."

He was silent for a long time, and I half-imagined the spirit of his mother at his shoulder, exerting her control.

"I was thinking that maybe he could spend a year with you," he said. "It might be hard for Michiko to take care of him and the baby, too."

My breath caught in my throat. Was he really saying this? It occurred to me that he was agreeing as a favor to his young wife. Maybe she didn't want to be reminded of Yusuke's former wife, the failed marriage that tainted her present one. Could it be that she was expecting a boy? I didn't care what the reason was. I felt sure that once I had him again, I wouldn't have to give him back. He could visit, of course. I wasn't going to cut him off from his father, but Kei belonged with me.

So now I'm at the airport, gazing at the sky. I see a pinprick of light, sun bouncing off silver, and I know that he is getting closer. It's only a matter of minutes before he steps off the plane and into the arrivals lounge. I'll hug him like a python, and then we'll go get something to eat. And when he's ready, I'm going to teach my son how to surf.

# About the Author

Suzanne Kamata was born and raised in Grand Haven, Michigan, and is most recently from South Carolina. She now lives in Aizumi, Japan, with her husband, bi-cultural twins, and mother-in-law. Her fiction and essays have been widely published and her work has been nominated for the Pushcart Prize five times. She is the editor of the anthologies, *The Broken Bridge: Fiction from Expatriates in Literary Japan* and *Love You to Pieces: Creative Writers on Raising a Child with Special Needs.*

ABOUT THE TYPE

This book was set in ITC New Baskerville, a typeface based on the types of John Baskerville (1706-1775), an accomplished writing master and printer from Birmingham, England. He was the designer of several types, punchcut by John Handy, which are the basis for the fonts that bear the name Baskerville today. The excellent quality of his printing influenced such famous printers as Didot in France and Bodoni in Italy. His fellow Englishmen imitated his types, and in 1768, Isaac Moore punchcut a version of Baskerville's letterforms for the Fry Foundry. Baskerville produced a masterpiece folio Bible for Cambridge University, and today, his types are considered to be fine representations of eighteenth century rationalism and neoclassicism. This ITC New Baskerville was designed by Matthew Carter and John Quaranda in 1978.

Composed by JTC Imagineering, Santa Maria,CA
Designed by John Taylor-Convery